WHAT IF IT'S EAS
EVERYTHING

VENUS
SHRUGGED

PART 1

DAN ANCONA

A NOVEL

VENUS SHRUGGED

PART 1

DAN ANCONA

Always forward.

CONTENTS

4

ISBN 978-1-365-95186-2

❈ Created with **Vellum**

For everyone, anywhere who gets involved.

But particularly for Jenifer.

And with special thanks to the Patron level crowdfunding supporters of this project:
Dale McGrew and Dan Girellini

She was warned.
She was given an explanation.
Nevertheless, she persisted.

Senator Mitch McConnell. February, 2017.

1

Oakland, California.
A few election cycles from now.

J ulietta Torres laughed.

The ramshackle campaign office normally had a bustle to it, but it broke through to a new level of haywire as half the desk and cell phones seemed to ring at once. Julietta had already spent too long on the phone with an unexpectedly thoughtful elderly supporter who'd sent them a check for $25 the day before.

Her donor went on, "Well, I have, to be honest. I first donated because I heard you talk about your family's story, and my family is from El Salvador too. I wasn't sure about you, though! This talk of reparations scared me a bit. But then I heard you talk about it and it did really make sense. And the early childhood education, housing, new trains, voting rights... I just love what you're talking about. Exactly what we need." Julietta smiled, relieved at the mention of some of the handful of issues their polling had surfaced after the ongoing debacle her early support for reparations had generated. The phone-ringing racket continued on in the background, and the voice on the phone asked, "What is all that, dear?"

"I'm sorry," she glanced up at the record in their donor database and paused (she hoped imperceptibly) "... Ms. Evans. It's been a pleasure chatting with you, but there's some kind of campaign mayhem occurring. I should probably look into it." Her tone remained charming as her brows scrunched together and she swept her dark brown hair off her shoulder behind the phone. Years of organizing had refined her intuition, and she was now crunching hard on something she couldn't quite identify but that left her with a strong and unmistakable sense that something was coming at them. Their primary so far against Steve Powell hadn't been particularly contentious: It was more like a conversation between two old friends who enjoyed talking political smack and had been at it for a long time. Not surprising, since that's exactly what they were.

So, maybe this was the shift, or maybe it was something else entirely. A negative story in the news, or something exploding and out of control on social media, or even just some kind of event planning or scheduling failure. And the million details a campaign was built out of could unravel at any moment. Julietta's mind wheeled through all the options as Ms. Evans politely shooed her off the phone.

Julietta had on her usual look, what her husband Doug dubbed "organizer chic": a ruffled, funky skirt, a loose white blouse, and a clockwork mechanism brooch. It was all locally made by a vendor she'd found on vacation at a hot springs a few hours north of Oakland a couple years earlier. She was barefoot. She had a pair of tall boots and a pair of flip flops next to her desk, which was otherwise empty apart from a battered laptop with its endlessly scrolling call lists, this morning's coffee cup, and one of the two-dozen fancy phones they'd rented. She slipped on the flip flops and leaned out of her office and around the corner.

The din seemed cheerful, even faintly ridiculous, and the happy chaos contrasted with the calm views out the seventh-floor plate-glass windows: clouds skimming/floating over the Oakland hills through a late summer haze kicked off the bay by the sea breeze. The interior furnishings of the office were comprised entirely of donated objects. Old computers along with laptops of every lineage sat perched on a mixture of desks, mostly fashioned from repurposed office doors held together with sawhorses. A few cocktail tables had been repurposed as standing desks. Her diverse staff of a dozen or so women and a few men was crowded around them, talking to each other as much as they were focused on the machines. When they'd narrowed down their choices of headquarters, the staffer who had gone to investigate described this one as "amazing view, smell not bad, carpets horrifying, plumbing seems functional." A slightly moldy tinge had never quite left the air, even after Julietta rented a steam cleaner one night before they moved in and pressed Doug into service to help her scrub it down; Doug in turn took the project over and managed to somehow recruit their six-year-old, Elijah, into helping while little Nora crawled around, hopefully improving her one-year-old immune system with whatever awfulness wound up in her mouth. The posters and historic campaign paraphernalia they'd covered the walls with didn't completely obscure the crumbling drywall. In a few places, the wood frames of the walls and wiring were visible. Julietta's office itself barely had room for her desk, the nicest and least funky of the donated couches, and a conference table they could just about get six people around. It would be home for them for only a few months, but it was homey enough.

Julietta's mood darkened when she noticed Felicia at her desk along the wall outside Julietta's office, underneath a sign that said simply, "CHANGE" with a small rising-sun Obama logo—Julietta's framed crowd sign from the 2008 Democratic Convention. Her beloved old friend and now campaign chief had a ferocious intellect coupled with a smile that could warm a small northern city in

January. But at the moment she was listening silently to someone on the other end of a phone while boring a hole into her laptop screen with her stare.

Julietta walked over to stand quietly behind Felicia, peeking over her shoulder at the screen. Felicia was scrolling down through the Sludge Report. It was not a site that had taken much of an interest in their race so far. Pacific Coast urban Democratic primaries were often the front lines of the battle between grassroots, racially diverse, more progressive Democrats and corporate establishment forces. Since Trump, these battle lines had intensified. As critical as they were for setting the direction of the party overall, they didn't tend to get noticed in the most extreme corners of the conservative media universe. Felicia noticed Julietta behind her and tried to shoo her away too, but when Julietta wouldn't budge, Felicia clicked on the snarky headlines anyway, written in Sludge's weird ellipsis-heavy style: "Bay Area Democrat 'Family Values'… Shocking New Pictures … Ties to infamous 'swinger church' Found …"

Julietta mumbled, "Oh no, not fruityfirst again," to no one in particular, but hoping it'd land somewhere in Felicia's direction, who kept ignoring her. Felicia didn't budge or look up as she scrolled down the page past pictures of Julietta that she recognized from a party. They were old, from maybe eight or ten years ago. Lovely shots that a friend of hers took, standing in front a glittery sign that said the name of the party they were at, "Sea of Kinky Dreams." There were a few pictures of her and Ayala, and then some pictures of her and Ayala and Kiyana, all in sheer lacey robes. Then a picture of her and Ayala smooching, then a picture of her and Kiyana smooching, then the three of them surrounding a sublimely happy looking Doug. Julietta's lips were pursed, sending the camera a little kiss, her brown hair longer then and up and messy behind her, while Ayala had a slightly goofy big smile, her huge brown eyes looking out from under a dark, almost-black tangle of curly bed-head. Kiyana was between the two, both smoldering and approachable, with dark skin, a big curly afro, and a smile more deep than broad and that radiated some kind of secret knowledge. Julietta had started dating Doug just a few months earlier, and the two of them had had their first date with Ayala maybe a week before this. Then the three of them went to the party together, where they met Kiyana for the first time.

The actual visual content of the pictures wasn't all that titillating, but she could see how the impression they transmitted—the clear, unmistakable sense that these were three dangerously empowered women—might have been, at least to certain audiences. If Sludge thought this was shocking, what happened the rest of the night would probably have required fainting couches for their entire newsroom. Julietta's happy memories collided with a sudden awareness of feeling exposed. She felt a wave of nausea that swept higher when she thought about Ayala and how this would affect her congregation.

Felicia finally mumbled "OK, thanks." She clattered the phone down, and looked up, and most of the tension was gone from her eyes. "No big deal, we knew this one was coming. Although..."

Julietta nodded, wanting her friend to go on.

"I don't know, Julietta. I warned you, at least. The whole thing about making things more difficult for yourself, right? This is it."

Julietta sighed. "I know, but what can I do?"

The campaign had made a deliberate decision not to try to do a thorough social media scrub for Julietta. She had planned early in her career never to run for office. It wasn't that she'd never wanted to be out front or had some preference for working in the trenches. It was simply that growing up mostly poor with a single mom, nothing much beyond that had seemed possible.

So, her social media footprint and trail of images was simply too large to deal with. When she'd decided running might actually be an option, her team reasoned that the times had changed, particularly in this district, and it would be at most a minor liability if some things got out. So they did what they could: They quietly tidied up the easy stuff, so at least someone would have to really spend some money and effort putting together an opposition, or "oppo," file, the playbook of sometimes-personal attacks that campaigns would use to structure their messages about an opponent. Then they'd written up an outline of a contingency plan as part of the campaign plan, printed it out (both out of tradition, and because a compromised network was one of the contingencies they had to anticipate), stuck it in a notebook, put it on a shelf, and hoped they wouldn't need it.

Now, six weeks out until voting started, they needed it.

The chaos bumped up another notch now with a fresh round of ringing phones. One of the new young staffers came over and handed her a cell phone and said, "I don't know what this is, but I think it might be a death threat." The young woman gulped and held the phone out. The phone wasn't on speaker, but it radiated awfulness anyway.

As Julietta met the woman's eyes she saw how scared the young staffer was: not shaking with it, but she was definitely affected. Julietta felt a brief moment of guilt at not being able to remember her name, but she touched her arm and said, "Don't worry. Thank you." She put the phone up to her ear. The male voice was loud and scratchy and indistinct, ranting and crackling in the little device's speaker. Julietta didn't talk, she just listened as it kept going. Among the words she could barely make out she caught a lot of "fucking" and "slut." Then some graphic descriptions of what the caller wanted to do to her and Ayala. At that she recoiled, the phone falling out of her hand as she jumped back. Her stomach knotted and flipped.

Lauren, their social media director, came over with another phone. It was the same kind of rant, maybe a recording she thought, although this one was in a different voice. Another wave of stomach knots hit her. Lauren started to hand the phone to Julietta, but Felicia grabbed it instead. Her eyes met Julietta's, and Julietta nodded. Felicia listened for a second, mashed the off button, and glowered at the phone.

Julietta looked at her and said, "Felicia, ah, we need to get the police and possibly the FBI on the phone. Let's go through the procedure." Felicia grabbed the folder off the shelf and started flipping through it.

Lauren's face contorted into. "OPD? Seriously? Wait. No. Stop." Felicia looked up from the pages.

Understanding flashed across Julietta's face. "Ohhh. Oh no. Right. Felicia, would you grab Henry? We have to talk, my office, now." She stopped and looked around the room at the faces looking to her. "No, wait. I need to talk to the staff first."

2

Julietta tried to steady herself and for a second felt like maybe she wouldn't be able to. It only took a few quick glances from the staff for her to confirm they needed to hear from her.

"Everyone, listen up for a second." Her voice trembled a little, but she waited for the quiet and for people to get off the phone and then continued less shakily. "As most of you know by now, our good friends at the Sludge Report have posted some pictures about me and some of my loves. And some of you have heard, we're getting death threats." The staff looked around the room, some moved nearer each other. "We have a procedure for dealing with this, and are going to start there. We're holding off on the police because I know a lot of you have history there, and because at this stage it's doubtful they'll be of much help anyway. We'll involve them if we decide together that we need to, and certainly no one will have to deal with them that doesn't want to. We don't need to panic. Unfortunately, as many of you have experienced, this kind of thing is not an uncommon occurrence on campaigns like ours. They think we're powerful and that's why they want to silence us. They're right about our power, but they are wrong about being able to stop us. Not happening." She took a deep breath. "We are a community and we're here for two things: to fight like hell for justice, and we keep each other safe while we're doing it. Part of that means standing up to bullies." The fear in the room hung there, she could still feel it. "Team, I believe in you. I believe in us. The jerks aren't going to win this one. Not today. If any other threats come in, record the times and the numbers and anything else you can. Pair up so you're not listening alone."

Then she said, "Lauren, Felicia, Henry, let's talk in my office." Henry was on the phone already but nodded. Just outside the door Julietta pulled Felicia over and asked her quietly, "This is your ship but mind if I run this meeting? Not so sure I want to." She thought for a second. "Actually I'm sure I don't want to. But I feel like it'd be better if I did. Lauren has some pretty intense personal history with the OPD."

Felicia whispered back to her. "I'm happy to handle it, I've got you. But I see your point." And then added, "I wouldn't say yes if I didn't think you had it in you. These guys are not getting inside our OODA loop. Not this time." Julietta laughed a little at her reference and remembered her and Doug discussing obscure warfighting theory years ago at dinner at their house. Observe, Orient, Decide, Act: the tactical decision-making process that every organization engaged in any kind of conflict went through. Julietta squeezed her old friend's hand in silent gratitude, for this moment and for the twenty years of their shared projects, campaigns, and friendship.

The four staff piled into her office. Henry was their combination research and political director. Julietta had met him years ago on a living-wage campaign. He grew up in West Oakland, spoke with a hint of his father's Jamaican lilt, was named after Henry Louis Gates, and was as passionate about granular policy details as he was about hearing the concerns of and holding together the leaders in their coalition. Lauren was the campaign's ebullient and disconcertingly sharp communications director. She had bright red chunky glasses

16

and a small tattoo of a stylized Port of Oakland crane on the left side of her neck, visible below the hair she usually kept shaved on that side. She'd been promoted almost instantly after getting hired to do social media, when Julietta overheard her gently but thoroughly fillet the arguments of a crusty old party insider who had suggested Julietta needed to wait her turn to run.

Julietta started out: "First, Lauren, are you OK?"

Lauren nodded imperceptibly and said to Julietta, "It's just this bind. I don't want us to not be safe. But I can't with the OPD. It's part of why I'm here." She looked up at Julietta, her face both pleading and defiant. Julietta nodded.

Felicia said, "We understand. I mean, you don't need to get into it. Or we can later if that'd be helpful. We're here for you." At this Lauren looked relieved. She said, "Thank you. I'd be happy to get into it sometime. It'd actually make me feel better to get into this and focus with you all."

Julietta said a silent prayer of thanks for finding people to work with who had this kind of toughness. "OK. Let us know what else you need if anything comes up. So, let's focus on everything else in the plan. Henry, did you talk to Sam already?" Sam was the sweet, aging doorman for their office building. The thought of something awful happening to him flitted through Julietta's mind, and she tightened.

Henry said, "Yeah, just talked to him. We're good. I didn't tell him everything that was up but just said to make sure to call us before letting anyone onto our floor."

Julietta said, "Great. Thank you. What about the four field offices?" They'd put real resources into their field operation and opened offices in all the corners of their district. "We have a few hours before the walkers go out. I say we give them all a day off. Paid. Lauren can you and Henry let the team leads know after this meeting?" They nodded. She went on, "If anyone has any other ideas or concerns about immediate physical security later today send them through Felicia or me. Felicia will own the plan for long-term security, after we get through this."

Julietta continued, "Alright, second point—anyone have evidence already that Powell or his team or anyone connected to them was behind this?" No one said anything. Josiah Carmulty, Powell's campaign manager, suddenly popped into Julietta's head, and she wondered if he was who her intuition had been chewing on earlier. "OK, let's assume he's not, for now, but let's get Carmulty on the phone and rake him over the coals just in case. Felicia, you got this?" Felicia shrugged but nodded. Julietta thought she noticed a little skepticism but kept going. "I doubt they're behind this. I honestly don't think they'd be smart enough even if they were evil enough. If you want to hint at some of the district family demographic research on him, do it, but don't tell 'em anything they shouldn't already know. If this is Powell trying to run a play he may be making a big mistake here. This could easily backfire on them."

Given the unusual structure of Julietta's family and some of her social circles, the campaign started out early running polling and deep research into the prevalence of alternative family structures in their district. The topics they covered ranged from multi-family communities sharing child care to woman-breadwinner households to single or co-parenting families to LGBTQ issues to open relationships. They ended up with a snapshot of the Bay Area family and relationship landscape, and even having lived it and studied it, they were shocked at the how rare the still-married heterosexual family norm was. Their intention wasn't ever to run on her family, or even to get them involved in any way so long as they could manage to avoid it. But Julietta had a hunch it was going to come up at some point, so they needed this data to plot out a defense.

The other tectonic undercurrent they picked up in their initial research was an overall level of abject economic misery. The brief, top-heavy recovery after the 2008 crash was slowly getting ground down due to a confluence of factors, but largely to housing prices and inequality that only spiraled upward. Unemployment was stuck at 10% district-wide and 18% in the city of Oakland, with roughly a third underemployed. Even the people with jobs were feeling squeezed. With unemployment that high, even highly paid workers felt completely replaceable. The long hours, brutal commutes, and widespread uncertainty that had only increased over the past few years were combining to make nearly everyone miserable.

Putting these things together—the old economic and family patterns failing, but the new ones not yet created—the campaign sensed an opportunity. They didn't stress it explicitly, but the core messages they crafted were all about addressing the baseline fears and frustrations generated by the crumbling of the old economic order.

In their initial rollout and press tour they'd stopped short of getting into the exact nature of her and Doug's relationship. They'd made a specific decision to deflect all questions on it, and it hadn't even come up. Now that the heat was on, with her and Powell locked into a close race, she supposed it wasn't entirely surprising that it had surfaced.

She continued, "Third question: Lauren, what's the reach of the story looking like?" Lauren looked up from her laptop and said, "It looks like the inoculation we did with our interviews with corporate media around this is holding up so far. Our Oakland Tribune contact actually texted me and said they weren't going near it."

Julietta said, "Well, that's amazing. Nice of him."

Lauren continued, "A couple California Tea Party and Trump blogs picked it up, and their Twitter is on fire and disgusting, of course, but you're probably getting as much of a boost from the sex-positive crowd as you are getting knocked down by the tea partiers. So far that's it. I have some ideas about how we could respond on the various channels though."

Julietta said, "My sense is that we have to be careful with that. If we respond and it gets picked up more widely, it could snowball and start generating more secondary impressions. More chance we'd get knocked off our positioning." She sighed and looked up the ceiling. "The thing I most want to avoid is becoming the 'sexy pictures candidate' rather than the 'antiracism candidate' and the 'public investment to create jobs candidate.'"

Lauren listened quietly. Julietta could tell she was waiting for an opening but went on, "I think the next step is research. I don't want to do a poll on this specifically, but maybe we should start our tracking polls early. We still have a little dough in the budget for some more focus groups, I hope? Let's watch the tracking and then quietly get inside people's heads on this as much as we can, particularly young women. I don't want to see our ones peeling off because of something we haven't thought of around this."

Henry nodded. A background in field organizing was a prerequisite for everyone Julietta hired, so when she referred to their "ones"—or their strongest supporters on the standard five-point scale —she didn't need to explain it to anyone in the room.

"OK, third topic: This friendly response that's coming in, what's that like? Henry, have you heard anything, or Lauren, you picking something up?" Lauren had been scrolling through the social media dashboard and looking at the custom machine learning and sentiment analysis tools that she'd cobbled together for them as an experiment. The set of programs she'd written sat on some cloud servers she'd spun up, constantly monitoring the online chatter in their district and popping up notifications and summaries for what was going on.

Lauren said, "We're not getting any organizational response yet. Just individuals. My guess is they are still crunching a response that's not going to hit us in the back. At least, I hope that's what they are thinking about. If you wanted to go on offense here, that'd certainly be possible. It would cue them on the right direction to go."

Julietta said, "I hear you, and I'm sure if anyone could run that kind of attack work, it's you. But I still think the possibility of blowing it up too much is too risky."

Henry had been spinning a pen in his hand in a way that seemed to both defy physics and magnify how fully absorbed in listening he was. He set the pen on the table and said, "Later this evening I'll make a couple calls, but we can probably expect at least Ultraviolet to light up their local list or maybe even statewide. They might be waiting to see what kind of legs it's got first, though. I'll come up with a list of other folks who might be willing to do a proxy counterattack." Ultraviolet was an online community with a national list of several million at this point. They could make a lot of noise, but they also had to be careful about the coordination laws constraining how they engaged politically.

Lauren chimed in, "The other group that could help us respond is Heartmob. Henry do you know anyone over there?" He shook his head. Heartmob was a fairly recent community of trusted anti-harassment activists. Lauren said, "I'm not sure they've worked with a candidate, but I can try them." She scribbled another note on the page she'd almost filled up.

Felicia said, "This question of how we respond publicly, if at all, is the five million dollar question here. I lean toward shooting back, generally. I think on general principles if a campaign doesn't respond to something like this, it looks like they can't take a punch or give one. Julietta's right about the danger of blowing this up a lot more hugely than it already is, if we start making a bunch of noise and go straight back at them."

Julietta thought for a second, her mind expanding out into all the ramifications of where this was heading. "What if we used the distributed field leadership? Felicia, I know we discussed this years ago, but have you ever tried it?"

Julietta's phone vibrated. She glanced at it and saw a text message from Doug: "what's up, i just got a kind of fucked up google alert about you." She looked up at everyone and said, "Hang on a sec, it's Doug." She wrote him back quickly: "yeah we're on it. in mtg now, don't worry, they're not in our ooda loop :) <3." Then added, "oh also could you let ayala know. ugh i feel awful about this, for her and for fruity1st." Fruity1st was their shorthand for the Fruitvale First Church of the Perennial Wisdom, the upstart warehouse church they'd been a part of for a few years.

She knew they'd be fine. This wasn't their first rodeo as far as scandals went. The previous big scandal was how Doug, Julietta, and Ayala first found out about Fruity1st a few years ago, and where the media's "swinger church" label had come from. Fox News had sent over a couple undercover reporters one morning when the message happened to include a few lines celebrating diversity of family, including non-monogamy. The resulting dust-up lasted a couple days on TV but was yet another backfire for Fox News: the coverage ended up growing the congregation by a factor of four over the next month, including Doug, Julietta, and Ayala after they saw the story. A few months later they'd grown enough to hire Ayala as their first rabbi and preacher.

She looked up and said, "OK, sorry. So, right, using field to respond." Her phone vibrated again, but she left it on the desk.

Felicia said, "We did, once. State house race in Virginia. Late mail hit called the guy a Nazi sympathizer because he'd been an ACLU member."

Julietta made a gagging noise. "Seriously?"

"Yup. He was a vet, too. Three tours in Afghanistan. The mailer had a big picture of a guy with a swastika tattoo. We lost, but it was the last weekend, and I'm not sure we had time to defuse it with our counterattack. So, it might work, but it takes a while. In this case we probably have time. Let me think about it but I'd probably be open to trying something."

Julietta said, "Lauren and Henry, can you two get together and draft an email to the neighborhood team leaders? I'll call some of the top folks myself to let them know what is up and help refine it from there. Actually—hang on a second." She stopped and stared at the ceiling again. "Something is bothering me here. Why is this happening?"

Blank stares from around the table. Julietta went on, "As far as conservative elections go, we're not even a backwater. No GOP candidate has a shot here, not even with the open primary. Why would somebody want Powell over me?"

The question hung in the room until Felicia said, "It's not about the election. This is a worldview play."

Julietta said, "How so?"

Felicia said, "I'm as big a fan of the economic plan that we've built as anyone; you know this. Linking reparations to universal basic income was a brilliant idea. I'm a little sad we're still not talking about it more, but I get it. And the issues we are talking about will make a big difference. I don't know if it's enough. You know my fears, that we're leaving a lot out and not connecting the dots on things well enough."

She took a breath and continued. "But none of that is a bag of chips compared to the family stuff. If the way you and Doug live starts to catch on, it's a direct threat to the parts of the economy feeding the 1%, which in turn is feeding the guys like Sludge. Hell, the racial composition of the people in that room," she nodded toward the campaign office, "is threat enough. Even since Trump, they know this."

Felicia kept going. "In fact, now that I think about it, these attacks could be about to get much worse. We need to be really careful here. It's easy to forget how unusual your life is because you two make it seem so easy and because of how you come across as so ordinary and approachable. I know it's hard for you both sometimes, like it is for everyone. It just doesn't look that hard, and that lack of shame makes you dangerous. The fact that you are connecting the family stuff with the economic plan and racial diversity, even in a vague way, even though we've made an effort not to go there too explicitly... just having these things connected might be scaring these guys on a fundamental level anyway."

Julietta looked concerned, but was nodding slowly as Felicia talked.

"In fact never mind what I said about worldview." Felicia leaned back, thinking it through. "The family stuff might be beside the point." She waved her hand, brushing it off. "It's really just about the bottom line, just about the bling. This stuff about investment in society, the stuff in your stump speech about culture and art and becoming a people-oriented, not thing-oriented society ... they know the only way to make that happen is with ongoing, big, government-run investments. Putting more wealth under democratic control. Which means taxes on them, and the only thing holding back our coalition is internal racism. We know this, and they know this. Every last bit of their argument comes back to keeping taxes low on rich folks. The only way to keep people focused on everything other than that is by playing them off each other. And the fact is, Powell is a hell of a lot less scary to them than you are on that. So someone, somewhere is willing to get ugly on us."

Julietta exhaled slowly. "I agree with all of that. But what do we do?"

Felicia said, "Whether we respond publicly is your call. Hate to say it." Julietta laughed a little at that, but frowned too. "I think we should respond, but I'm not kidding myself about the risks, either. There are things we can do even if we don't respond directly. Let's try Heartmob, Henry can talk to some of the other groups, and letting the field organizers know to look for this and how to fight back seems worth trying."

24

Julietta said, "That sounds like a good plan. Hold off on talking to the field organizers though, for now."

Felicia spputtered a bit. "We have to tell them something. It's going to start coming up in our conversations. We don't want our organizers to hear about this first when someone texts them back a link to it."

Julietta said, "I get that. I just don't think it's gone that big yet. How many people in our district read Sludge? It rounds to zero. This is how I want to leave it for now."

Felicia was clearly annoyed, but Julietta ignored her smoldering irritation. "I'm grateful for all of you today. Don't make me say the Seneca line." Lauren smiled at her and cut her off: "Fate leads the willing and drags the unwilling!" Julietta laughed. "This is why we built this campaign the way we did. Let's see what it can do. Can you two give Felicia and me the room?"

As Lauren and Henry filed out, Julietta slumped into her chair. Felicia gave her a concerned look as Julietta said, "Felicia, this is really freaking me out. I'm worried it hasn't even really hit me yet."

"Yeah, seems like it."

"Thanks." She groaned quietly and the stress and anger seemed to hang hazy in the air, but then, for no apparent reason, it seemed to dissipate a little.

Felicia said, "You up for talking a little more about this?"

"Honestly, I'm not. I don't want to drag the staff through this if we have to. Like I said, if we need to change direction, we will."

Felicia was silent but sensed a dead end. She didn't want to crash into it, at least not yet. "OK. Think it through, because I have a bad feeling about where this is headed. Anything else you need?"

"I'm not even sure. I just can't wait to get home and hug Elijah and Nora."

Felicia nodded. "How are they doing?"

Julietta said, "Oh you know. They miss their mama. Well, at least

Elijah does. Being six is hard. It's kind of killing me. Nora doesn't really seem to notice, she mostly just giggles and sings to herself."

At that moment Lauren knocked and Julietta gestured for her to come in. "Felicia, it's one of the media buyers. Want me to brush him off again?"

Felicia looked at her friend, "You good for now?"

Julietta said, "Yeah, yeah. Go deal, I'm OK."

Alone again, Julietta kicked off her flip flops and leaned back in the creaky old wooden chair they'd found in the storage unit a local party club had let them browse through. She thought back to the Burning Man years ago where she'd first met Steve Powell. Maybe this was it. Maybe Powell was going to win. It wouldn't be an immediate disaster, but it would be yet another progressive failure. Powell winning would be yet another setback for the political movement she'd dedicated her life to, the only hope she had for her country to beat back the increasingly scary challenges more and more Americans were facing every day.

Steve and Julietta's rambling, dusty conversations then were all visions for the future and how to connect the explosively creative and positive energy they felt out there with the reality of their lives. Back in 2000 it all seemed impossibly far apart, incredibly distant. Later that year they both worked on a living-wage campaign, before Powell went off to build a startup that turned out successfully enough that he was able to almost self-fund his campaign, along with a few of his venture capitalist pals. These weren't bad guys, mostly; Julietta knew a lot of them, and they at least kept a veneer of being open-minded and forward-looking. But she had certainly run into a nasty vein of privilege and sexism right below the surface in some of them at times when their paths had crossed. After not being invited to enough events over a period of years (the reasons changed every time, but curated was a word that came up a lot), she'd drifted farther from his crowd and, the Bay Area being the Bay Area, had easily found more inclusive circles of friends.

Running had forced both of them to define their visions, and those visions diverged. They started out without much daylight between them, but as the nature of the campaign forced them to draw contrasts, she was disappointed to watch Powell give up so much of what his core vision had been. He almost gave up arguing for it at all. He went beyond just tamping down the original, more fiery, vision of economic transformation that Julietta knew they shared and veered into making arguments that were comforting but counterproductive. She understood the bet that the electorate would, yet again, lean older and more conservative, but she thought it was hollow strategy. The point of leadership for her wasn't to just meet people where they were at and leave them there. It was to move them!

Powell had always been somewhat moved by the kind of progressive-sounding libertarian arguments that another of their campmates from back then, Peter Dixon, had made. Dixon had also gone on to build a successful banking startup. Julietta wasn't sure, but at times felt like she could hear Dixon's arguments in Powell's message. She'd read that Dixon had been working with a libertarian Republican presidential campaign but wondered if he and Powell were still in touch.

Julietta hadn't made concessions so much as she'd honed the language, refined her argument, and narrowed the range of issues she focused on, instead of giving up anything substantive. The arguments about language weren't her primary expertise—she was much better at the tactical stuff—but her campaign staff, Doug included, relished this process and stayed up many nights arguing the finer points and boiling down arguments to their most potent essences. But through all the sophisticated machinery, she still allowed the fire to come through at times. Their message of antiracism as the path forward was one that resonated. It worked. They needed that fire to reach young people. By coloring inside the lines of the older electorate, Powell didn't. She wasn't convinced it was even a winning strategy: She had no shortage of older white supporters who were right there with her when she brought the fire. Powell's was an easier path to victory, but for Julietta, winning the easy way wasn't worth the trouble of running.

The possibility of taking the harder path and having it result in a victory was ultimately what persuaded to her to make the run. Like the rest of their staff, Doug and Julietta started their political careers years ago doing field organizing: the volunteer recruitment, knocking on doors, personal contacts and long-term relationship and organization development that had, along with social media, gradually replaced print mail and TV ads as the meat and potatoes of the campaign world over the past few cycles.

Julietta didn't know it at the time, but the seeds for her campaign had been planted back in the days of the living-wage campaign she'd worked on. The coalition that generated it was a group of unions and economic and social-justice affinity groups. They were entirely unaffiliated with the Dem party or with local electeds; they'd protested more than gone to meetings. But over time their tactics changed, and Julietta and Doug had both worked to build bridges into the party through a series of local Democratic Party clubs. So, now there was a outside-to-inside continuum of organizations, and activists could plug into the network wherever they felt most comfortable.

The hope was that this would be a more resilient, agile, and powerful structure for a campaign, but they also felt that, even if they lost, their hard work at engaging these voters would leave the East Bay structure of democracy better off and more participatory than it was before. When Julietta and Doug first got involved they'd thought a campaign as a tool for improving democracy was at least a theoretical possibility, but now here they were, building and running just such a thing, built on the principles of respect, empowerment, and inclusion that the Obama campaign had started out with in 2008.

28

They were really getting to know the people who were leading their teams in the neighborhoods. They'd built up a degree of trust. The volunteers down to the block level felt like they were part of the team since they had inside knowledge of what was going on. Julietta's campaign was essentially recreating a vastly more inclusive version of early twentieth-century American democracy with fancier communications networks and in the most gloriously diverse piece of political turf anywhere. Just over 300,000 Democratic voters, and unfortunately as segregated nearly everywhere else: white folks mostly up in the hills with people of color down in the flats, with a few more slightly integrated neighborhoods in the middle. Despite this, it was an incredibly, beautifully diverse district, where more races and creeds were represented than anywhere else in the country. And unfortunately, vast barriers of inequality that separated their lives so far from each other. But this campaign was built to smash those barriers: The whole thing was built to drive power, dignity, and respect down and out into the community she'd adopted twenty years ago and grown to love so deeply.

Amazingly, it was all working. But the screaming, nasty voice on the phone from the afternoon came back to Julietta suddenly. She wondered about what she'd missed, about what larger forces might be in play that could have leaked the pictures and led to this. Felicia once told her that her superpower was the ability to understand the motivations of everyone in the room at once and to pick the right path through all of them.

She started thinking about the motivation of the person at the other end of the line screaming obscenities at her but quickly stopped, shivering a bit at what else someone like that might be capable of. She wondered if, or when, they were going to find out.

3

The next morning when she arrived back at the office, there was a Post-It note on top of her messages with a giant hand-scrawled red arrow pointing to one of them. She had a brief moment of love for her staff, followed by a sharp attack of concern over what would have driven one of them to take a step like that. Had she spaced on calling some guy back; was he freaking out?

The message was just a name, Rafael Somos. Not just a big donor, one of their two or three biggest. He and his father had both maxed out their contributions but their true value was vastly greater than that: They'd probably singlehandedly recruited two dozen or so other large donors to her campaign. Julietta had met him a few years ago, and they worked together a bit as the D12 Alliance donor network was getting started. She'd orbited the donor network world for a few years and saw the good they could do, as well as the array of challenges and limitations that you might expect from several hundred people, diverse across every axis except wealth, attempting to coordinate strategy on just about anything.

Rafael was good-looking, if in a slightly bland, traditional way, and a little younger than her. As she watched him participate in the

Alliance, she thought he seemed to be navigating better than most the world of incredible privilege that had been handed to him. They were on a first-name basis but not much beyond that, but when she announced her campaign his check arrived a few days later, entirely unsolicited. His father had made their family unimaginable, mind-shearing amounts of money the way people usually did in the 1980s: through real estate, hedge funds, and then currency speculation. But Rafael had recently founded a chain of healthy fast-food restaurants called Get Saucy that was growing explosively. She was surprised to hear he had any energy to think about politics.

She held up the Post-It. "Lauren, this one you?" She nodded. "How did I know? What's up?"

"He sounded a little … agitated."

"Oh, goody. He say anything about why?"

"Said he was concerned about Sludge and that he wanted to talk to you directly before he said more."

Julietta said, "Hm. OK, thanks. Felicia, what do you think, want to plot strategy on this?"

Felicia looked up from her laptop. "He probably just needs to be talked off the ledge a piece, right? If he's just having a feeling, don't spend too much time on it. Lots of other shit that needs doing today."

Julietta said, "I hope that's all it is."

She went back to her office and dialed him.

"Julietta, hello."

"Rafael, good to hear from you. I imagine this is related to yesterday's exemplary journalistic integrity from our friends over at the Sludge Report?" She was taking a risk diving in with a little snark but hoped it would help take the edge off his concerns, whatever they were.

"Not just, but yes. I'm … curious, let's say, about some of the decisions that your campaign has been making." She tightened at the way he put it but didn't say anything. "It's as much about your economic plan as what Sludge wants to throw around. You seem like you've gone a bit past where D12 is at on some of your economic thinking."

This wasn't what she expected. Defending the economic messaging wasn't her strong suit, but she decided to plunge in. "Well, you're right. We tested some of the more incremental Alliance messaging early on and it wasn't working for our people. Not here. You probably saw it's substantively the same, we've just narrowed it down to a few issues and with a little more passion in the delivery. The way we're putting it seems to be working in reaching our base. And we really needed to differentiate from Powell."

Not satisfied with that and sensing he wasn't either, she went on, "I have a great team researching this. I trust them." It was the truth but she twitched a bit inside at how it might have sounded: like she wasn't taking full responsibility.

"I see. Well, our concerns, beyond wondering about the effectiveness and substance of what you're proposing, were that you had amped up the rhetoric around inequality a bit too much. We believe it's possible to make this argument without demonizing anyone."

The "our" in what he said fairly jumped out at her, but she wasn't sure if that was him and his Dad, or the Alliance, a faction inside the Alliance, or someone else. She tried to keep the edge of exasperation she was feeling out of her voice and asked neutrally, "What exactly about it is troubling you?"

"We can get into specifics if you'd like, but it was more just a general concern about the tone. And it wasn't just me that was concerned. A couple other Alliance members have reached out to me."

That was it, then. It was a faction. She was stunned, and momentarily even a bit flattered, that they were paying so much attention. Or any attention at all. She wanted to get into numbers:

How many of the D12 was still with her and how many had she lost. But then she had a brief moment of amazement that Rafael and some unknown number of his allies were still with her. And that enough were still with her for him to stick his neck out and try calling.

As badly as she wanted to know the details of what was going on, she quickly realized that whatever her position was, giving him the best tools she could to defend her was going to be a better use of her time. She said, "I see. To be honest, we do have an element of negativity in there. Our research found that starting with that was really the only way we could open the door to some of our target demographics. And that if we didn't start there we were perceived as not credible. However, if you look at how we've been structuring how we're talking about it, we transition hard to the positive vision and what a more democratized economy would look like as quickly as we can. I'd say we've been relentlessly focused on that." She wondered if she could get away with changing the subject. "What were your substantive concerns?"

Rafael bit and said, "How to best put this. Let's say it's the consensus of D12 that we are skeptical, or at least not yet so convinced, that the public investments in infrastructure, the arts, and science like the ones you're calling for are remotely politically feasible —at this moment. We love science, space, and energy as you do, but we think talking about NSF, NASA, and NREL probably isn't the most effective first step. People know NASA, but the National Science Foundation is continually mired in controversy, and no one's ever heard of that National Renewable Energy Lab."

Another wave of irritation. There were so many ways to go with this, she wasn't exactly sure where to start. She suppressed the urge to them him that's exactly the problem she was trying to fix and instead said, "Well, you'll be glad to know we've tightened our focus and are mostly sticking to infrastructure now. Housing and transportation, the nuts and bolts stuff is just generally more resonant." But something else was bugging her so she decided to press him. "Is the D12 on the record saying this anywhere? And this is the consensus of the whole group, or the subset of the group that reached out to you?"

"Good questions, and no, this is not on the record."

Julietta said, "Well, I get it. This is a tough sell. But unemployment is nearly 20% in Oakland. A third underemployed districtwide. We have to fund good jobs. I don't know another path. The private sector is growing here, just not fast enough. And it's not like one grows without the other. They're inextricably linked."

Rafael said, "You've had your own economists go over this?"

She shot back, "Of course. A lot of the core ideas are based on Roosevelt and INET plans"—the Roosevelt Institute and the Institute for New Economic Thinking, both of which many of the D12 members had funded—"and as I said, I trust my policy team as much as my political folks." She hated going back to her reliance on others for this, but she wasn't sure how else to reach him or what else might validate their approach.

"I see." She couldn't tell if he was familiar and just not supportive of INET or if he was unaware. But she was getting more nervous the longer the conversation went this direction, so she didn't raise the question. He sighed slightly, and something seemed to shift for him. With a new trace of warmth, he said, "Julietta, I hope you know, we're not trying to quarterback from the sidelines here."

She was silent, considering. He said, "Really, I mean it. We want to figure this out as badly as you do. Or at least, some of us do."

Again she felt the faction there, felt the potential opening. She said, "Maybe if I sent you some of the research we came up with? Or put you in touch with our contacts at the think tanks?"

"That would help, I think. And just so you know, my personal concerns are very limited here. In fact I think you give a hell of a speech. But I felt like there was a need for someone to run a bit of interference for you, and I volunteered to take point on it."

"Well, I appreciate that. I'll get you my INET and Roosevelt contacts, and we can get some of the raw focus group data out to you as soon as we wrap up."

"Thanks, I do think that will help. Now, I am also concerned about these Sludge attacks. I have to admit, your family structure is a bit of a surprise to me. It wouldn't have affected mine or the rest of my family's investment if we'd known, but we did feel like this is something of a curve ball." Her body clenched at this; she could only think that what he meant by this was that they bloody well never would have cut her a check if they knew she and Doug had an open relationship back when they didn't mind people taking pictures of them. She wondered how many other large donors were contemplating swinging to Powell or sitting this primary out over this.

But they'd practiced for this, so instead of getting more irritated she snapped onto the argument they'd crafted in their contingency planning. "I understand, and I hope you know that our motivation in not being more up-front was not about hiding anything. First, we are taking a clear stand in favor of discretion. We felt we couldn't be logically arguing for greater personal privacy but not taking advantage of it ourselves, even as a public figure. Second, we very badly wanted the campaign to be about our economic vision and substance. I know all candidates say this, but I believe our team is entirely focused on this part of the project."

Rafael was listening quietly but she sensed somehow that this was working, so she went on.

"We didn't think Powell would make an issue out of this, for various reasons. Partially because I've known him for a long time and I know how he operates. But given the stakes, we did think it might come up, either from him or someone else. So, I'll bring you on the inside on something, if you'd like. I realize this is a nontrivial request but I'd prefer for the Alliance not to know about what I'm about to tell

36

you, at least for now. Since we're not sure what do with it yet ourselves."

He was quiet, thinking. Then he said, "I can do that, provisionally at least. Say until after the campaign?"

"That should be fine. We have someone research showing that, were it to come out, our family structure may actually cut both ways for us. At least in this district. There was vastly more support for and openness to it than we anticipated, at any rate. We couldn't afford nearly the level of research we wanted to get to really understand this effect and get inside it, but we did enough to at least take an educated guess that if it did come out, it wasn't going to torpedo us."

"That's fascinating news. And I'm glad to hear you're taking such a deliberate approach with the research."

She said, "Thank you. I know I keep talking about them but this team is really something. I'm lucky to have them. I hope you'll understand if I don't send that report along at least for now."

"Certainly, but I hope we can continue the conversation after the election."

"Happy to, of course. I'm sure you're busy. But I hope you know we're big fans of Get Saucy here in the office."

"Thanks! I'm genuinely glad to hear it. It's been quite a ride so far. Not what I was expecting out of this life."

She said, "I understand that feeling. A lot." She felt a little murmur of connection, empathy for him. Not at all what she was expecting from how the call started.

"Well, thanks for calling, and I appreciate your help with the D12 folks. I'll make sure we get the focus group and INET and Roosevelt deep research out to you."

"Thanks, Julietta. Hope to talk more soon."

"Me as well, hopefully at our victory party."

"Sounds good!"

The phone had barely clicked before her head was poked out the door. "Lauren, could you get a copy of the last two econ message focus groups and the last poll, pull it together, and email it from my account to Rafael? And send him some of the INET policy briefings, just the summaries. Make sure there's nothing about the family structure and LGBTQ stuff in it; that's internal only still. And Felicia, we gotta talk."

Felicia came in and pulled the door behind her. "How'd it go?"

Julietta exhaled deeply. She said, "I think the call went OK but the Alliance could be kind of a problem. We should probably get a cross-reference of how many of them are supporting Powell. They aren't happy with how we've been turning up the heat."

Felicia said, "You told them people won't even open the door for us if we don't add that, I hope."

Julietta said, "Yeah. I have no idea if it made sense to him. He seems like not a bad guy, although who knows what the other D12ers are saying to him." She tapped her fingers on her desk, starting to count up who might be for and against them.

Felicia said, "Oh, the delicious irony of it. The people leading the innovation on economic thinking are giving us a hard time for talking about economics. He didn't happen to mention their better ideas on fixing unemployment or talking to voters about it, did he?"

Julietta laughed. "Of course not. Why would they do that when they can just throw some rocks at our windows instead." She sighed. "This makes me nervous as hell. I don't want to piss these people off, for a bunch of reasons, but I also don't want them shaping our game too much. Maybe what I gave Rafael is enough for them to leave us alone for a bit."

Felicia said, "Worth trying at least. Julietta, there's one other thing we need to go over."

Julietta guessed what was coming but said, "What's that?"

"I think we need to brief the field team to counterattack on Sludge, as soon as possible."

"You don't think that's going to blow it up worse? I've been having serious second thoughts on even going that far."

Felicia sensed a wave of fear in her friend. "I don't. I think it's out there. I don't think it's healthy to not respond, and if we're going to respond we want to do it sooner rather than later."

Julietta said, "Maybe I'm spooked over this call from Rafael, but I think we should wait. For now. We still have time to respond if it gets worse. If the donors bolt, we're screwed."

Felicia seemed to be getting impatient. She said, "If you don't trust my hunch on this, what about the data? I looked at the notes from our canvassers at doors and over texts, and it has been coming up."

Julietta narrowed her eyes and said, "I do trust your hunches generally. How many times has it come up?"

Felicia hesitated and said, "About ten in the past week, with a couple references to it that seemed like they might have had something to do with it."

"Ten. Out of how many contacts?"

"Over the past week we had just over 7,000."

Julietta stared at her. "Ten. Out of 7,000."

"I know it doesn't sound like that much. But for every person who actually mentioned it there's probably a hundred that know about it. And we don't have that much time. You know you don't technically need the big donors at this point, right?"

Julietta said, "I'm pretty sure that's not true. Did our small donors tick up finally?"

"No, not really. It's been hard to get them off the dime for a local race, as we expected. Even yours. But I looked at the budget. We could cut more TV."

"Felicia, Powell will shred us on TV if he senses an opening. It's not where our base is, I know, but if we get destroyed in the hills we're not going to be able to make it up in the flats. We have to fight him to a draw up there. I know we're guessing he won't go negative,

39

but what if he does? If our fundraising slacks more it'd be borderline political malpractice not to."

Felicia said, "Our ones are holding so steady, though. A couple TV ads aren't going to knock them off. And we're crushing him in the field. We sent one of our top volunteers over to check out his volunteer operation and it was deserted. Purely cosmetic."

Julietta stared out the window. "That's great to hear, but I still don't know. My hunch is saying it will be too risky and it's going to blow over. That's my call for now."

Felicia sighed. She didn't seem sure how far to press it. "I think we're making a mistake."

Julietta said, "I get that."

Then Felicia added, "Well, it's possible in the end it won't matter. If our people show up, we still have this."

Julietta said, "Thanks, love. I hope so."

The first thing Felicia did when she got back to her desk was to quietly prepare the plan to fire back. Just in case they needed it.

4

Truly hot, 90- or 100-degree days are rare enough in the Bay Area, and unfortunately enough for anyone working on a campaign, they largely occur during October. Ayala was deeply determined to celebrate this one. She slipped on a pair of running shorts and a dark blue yoga top that she guessed would show off her four-months-pregnant belly and her shoulders equally well, and tied her mass of curly hair up and back into a huge ponytail. She was going to need an unusually persuasive look to accomplish her goal of kidnapping Julietta today.

She went downstairs. Doug had already corralled the four kids to the breakfast table, with one-year-old Nora in her chair, five-year-old Avi playing with a small yellow toy backhoe and pushing cereal around in his bowl, six-year-old Elijah giving his sister little scraps of his toast. Max and Ananda's kid, ten-year-old Alexander, was wolfing down the second of three eggs. It was their ordinary morning scene of mostly managed chaos.

"Morning, loves!" She stood in the doorway of the kitchen, and Doug glanced over from the dishes, and said a low "Yow" when he looked up and saw her. He turned the water off, walked toward her while glancing back at the momentarily calm herd of eating kids, and quietly dragged her around the corner.

Doug had no idea why, but exercise clothes turned him on more than just about anything else. The traditionally sexy stuff—lace panties and the rest of it—were fine, but nothing did it for him like a yoga top visible under a transparent workout T-shirt. Ayala and Julietta were both greatly amused by the situation and didn't hesitate to play it up for him and had even both come around to agree with him. So, now he pushed her up against the wall lovingly, kissed her neck slowly and ground his body gently into her. She moaned as he ran his fingers over her shoulders and down her back, feeling her insides melt and her excitement for him starting to build. Unlike her first pregnancy, this time she'd been almost relentlessly turned on. It had simmered during her first trimester and increased over the past month to the point of being a near constant distraction.

All of which was interrupted by the entirely predictable crash from the kid table. He whispered to her, "Nothing turns me on more than seeing you like this." They looked back in to see the plate Nora had pushed off her tray with Elijah cleaning it up. He looked over at him, "Daddy, Nora just pushed her food off but don't worry, I got it." Ayala and Doug grinned inwardly at his six-year-old helpfulness. "Thanks, pal! You rock." Doug called and returned his focus to the crazed lust he was feeling for Ayala, but knowing the clock was ticking on the morning scramble, said to her, "What are your plans today, all dressed up sexy like this?"

She said, "I thought I'd go and see if I could free your wife from Felicia's clutches. It's a gorgeous day, things are reasonably calm at church, and I know this Sludge Report situation is dragging on her. What do you think?"

Doug said, "You've got a lot more pull with Felicia than I do. Worth a try." He thought for a second. "I have an idea for you, too: Remember the thing we talked about last time we were up off that trail in Redwood? Want me to go set it up?"

Her face lit up. "Doug love, that is genius. Today is perfect for that. You sure you can?"

Doug said, "I shouldn't blow off work, but I can. I'll work tonight. Let's do it. I'll send you the description of the location and GPS coordinates once I've got it set up. I can bring Nora with me in the backpack for the setup even. She loves looking at the redwoods."

She laughed a little, "Whoa, are we really doing this?"

He said, "Yes! Sure! Come on, we have to try it."

Max and Ananda hurried into the kitchen from their room upstairs. Max was tall and bald, with intense, piercing blue eyes, but was almost always smiling. Ananda had dark eyes and dark hair and a curvy, medium build, her family's South Indian influences clear. She said brightly, "Morning, you two!" then looked Ayala up and down, emitted a little growl, and gave her a squeeze and said, "You're looking cute. Off to catch the bus!" They both kissed Alexander on the head then slipped out the door as he said, "Bye Mom, Bye Dad!"

Ayala herded the big kids into the minivan and dropped Avi, Elijah, and Alexander off at school then drove to the storefront field office she knew Julietta was working out of that day, down in Fruitvale, as Doug quickly assembled a sheet and their queen-sized camping mattress and dug into a closet for a couple pieces of red, gauzy cloth. Looking back into the kitchen he grabbed a pitcher, two glasses, a tray, a lemon, a cucumber, and filled a water bottle full of water, threw it all in a duffel bag, then grabbed the kid backpack and said to Nora as he picked her up, "Come on, sweet pea, we are going to go build mommy a nice surprise."

Ayala parked and walked into the office finding Felicia drawing shapes on a big map of the district on her screen.

Ayala said, "Hi, Felicia. What's up? Cutting turf?" Felicia nodded and was friendly as they hugged but also a bit guarded; Felicia loved Julietta's whole extended family, Ayala included, but this wasn't the first time Ayala had shown up at the office unannounced to borrow Julietta for a break. Since it was Felicia's job to keep Julietta focused, a little tension filtered inevitably through her greeting.

Ayala said, "It's too hot and gorgeous out to be in an office today."

Felicia smiled, "Yep, that's why we're going knocking later. Want to come with us? Got some choice precincts up by the compound that haven't been done yet."

"You're going to make the pregnant lady walk the hills, are ya!"

"Come on, you know you are our deadliest weapon at the door. How many contacts did you get last week, 30 in a couple hours? Unheard of."

"Hmm, I guess I do have an unfair advantage." Ayala was feeling a little close to being talked into this so hurried to change the subject, "Where's the boss lady at? I need to, ah, borrow her for a little while. Not for long. And I'll think about coming with tonight, at least for a bit." She came closer to Felicia. Voice low she asked, "How's she doing? I'm worried about this Sludge Report crap." She gave another little growl.

"To be totally honest, I'm worried too. Outwardly she seems pretty unshakeable. You should have seen her when it came in; she took over the meeting and was quiet and confident and flawless with just the right amount of vulnerability. The staff knew it was hitting her and was a big deal but that it wasn't going to throw us. Good stuff, even by her standards."

"Aw, I can imagine. I love that side of her. So, what's worrying you?"

Felicia said, "Eh, I don't know. Just caught her spacing out a couple of times, and she seemed pretty freaked out when we talked afterwards. And, she doesn't want to respond."

Ayala said, "Is that a mistake? I don't know how these things work."

"Hard to say. Maybe, but maybe not. I definitely made the case for

44

it. I see her side of it, but it's been a couple of days and it doesn't seem to be going away." Felicia hesitated, almost imperceptibly. "If you wanted to ask her about it that might not be a bad idea. You don't have to pressure her one way or the other, just hear her out."

Ayala said, "I think I can handle that."

Felicia said, "I don't know if it's possible to not be shaken up on some level by an attack like this. Did she tell you about the thing with Rafael and the D12?"

Ayala shook her head. "The donor group? I've heard of them, but no, she didn't mention anything."

"You should ask her about that, too. I'm on board with you doing a little kidnapping. Five more weeks is both no time at all and a long time to keep trucking at the pace she's on." Felicia nodded toward the rear of the office. "She's in the back."

Julietta was on the phone, smiling. She was quiet, listening, but she got up and came over and hugged Ayala close, gently running one hand over her belly and the other along her shoulders and then up her neck and through her hair. Ayala could hear a voter unloading on her, but from what she could hear, the person was more excited than irritated.

Julietta put her hand over the mic and said, "Small donor. I love these calls." Then back into the mic she murmured a couple agreeable, "mmmmhmmms" before wrapping it up and focusing finally on Ayala. She leaned over and closed the door to Julietta's office and gave her a long, slow kiss hello before pulling back and saying, "Hi! I am SO glad to see you!"

Ayala said, "Clearly!" First Doug and now her. This was turning out to be a nice morning. "I don't have any clients until this afternoon, and I am here to kidnap you. Felicia is even on board, so no complaining. We're headed for the woods for a hike."

"Sounds great, but…" Julietta looked over at the desk and the laptop with its scrolling pages of names she needed to call. "I just can't. Plus I have nothing to wear." Ayala produced a change of clothes out of her bag, rabbit-out-of-a-hat style. "Doug set me up. Come on. You heard me that Felicia was even on board, right? This one's guilt free. You can't be fighting for everyone to work less hard and work as hard as you have been, love. It doesn't make any sense."

Julietta relented. "OK, OK. Where are we going?"

"I don't even know yet," Ayala answered mostly honestly since Doug hadn't texted her. "Let's just get out of here. Here, I can be helpful." She started fingering the buttons on her blouse but then stopped for a second, their eyes locked, breathing quietly together. Ayala started undressing her slowly, running her hands over Julietta's chest and pulling her blouse out of her skirt and down off her shoulders. Her bra and chest now exposed, Ayala pulled Julietta toward her. Julietta started to respond: She turned Ayala around and leaned her over with her hands on the desk, feeling her hips from behind, moving her hand under her. Julietta felt her turn on, accelerating fast, but stopped herself and said, "OK, no wait; this is not a good idea. We have enough scandal in this office already! Let's get out of here. You're right. I need the break. Give me those clothes, will ya."

"OK, I'm going to pee, then let's go." Ayala slipped past Julietta and out of her office, feeling a flush in her cheeks as a raft of adorable young campaign workers looked up at her with curious, half-knowing smiles on their faces. She quickly texted Doug but before she'd even sent the "???" he shot back, "Perfect spot, found a fairy circle next to a trickling stream 100 yds off starflower trail, 0.3 mi up from the bottom of the hill, turn right at small cairn and go up the hill" and a latitude and a longitude. Ayala grinned to herself. A second later "p.s. leave the stuff when you are done, I will come back for it."

Ayala texted back, "You're the best, thank you <3 <3 <3!!1!!"

5

A s soon as they were in the car, Ayala felt Julietta's body unwind itself. Julietta took in a deep breath. "OK, I really needed to get out of there. Thank you."

Ayala put her hand on Julietta's knee, slowly ran it up her leg and looked over at her, smiling. Shivers ran up both their bodies. "Happy to. I've been a little worried about you."

Julietta said, "I've been a little worried about you too! Although you seem like you're doing great. And Doug is being adorable with you. He was exactly the same way when I was pregnant with Elijah and Nora. It's making me really happy to see it again. I wasn't expecting it."

"You sure it's OK? You don't miss it being you? It's sure a different experience for me. Although it is making me nostalgic for things with Owen, in some weird way."

"Really!"

Ayala said, "Yeah—despite our issues, he was amazing, too, and I see that amazingness in Avi every day. I'm glad he's happy. I wasn't sure if the way things worked out, with me having another kid with you guys, was going to be hard for him. But he's changed a lot. Owen,

I mean. Although Avi too."

"Truth. When he and Doug went out with all the kids the other night, he seemed great. And to answer what you asked about missing it … oh holy sweet mercy, no, I sure don't." Julietta laughed a little. "I thought I would! I thought it would be a lot harder than it's been, I really did. But I seem to have my hands full. Mostly I'm grateful for all your help with the kids. And for keeping Doug distracted while I'm working this hard."

"Yeah, so about that. How's it going?" Julietta was quiet. "The Sludge thing is a little intense. You doing OK?"

"Oh, you know." She stared out the window. "Fuck Sludge. Seriously." Ayala thought there was more, though, so she kept quiet. Julietta continued, "But, yeah. I do keep thinking about it. The death threats and the bullshit tidal wave we are getting online has been rough at times. And now the donors are getting a little spooked."

Ayala said, "Yeah, Felicia said something vague about that."

"I don't know how big of a deal the donor thing is. They sent the guy I have the best relationship with to call me. I like him, and I think I pretty well smoothed it over. The staff is doing the best they can to insulate me from the worst stuff online, but I've looked at the raw feeds myself a couple of times. It's ugly. I'm not sure I get where it's coming from, really."

"I do," said Ayala.

"You do? What do you think is going on?"

"I think you're a bigger threat to the order of things than you realize. Or at least you're perceived that way."

Julietta considered this. "It's so strange to me. We're hardly proposing anything radical. Probably the most challenging thing we are doing is defending the role of government at all, in terms of our message."

"It's not about your message, it's about your identity, and your family. Me, to some degree. Even fruity1st, to some degree."

Julietta felt a stab of guilt at dragging her family community into it. "Ugh. That makes me feel awful. Ayala, why am I doing this?"

Ayala squeezed her thigh. "Because we want you to! We're tough. We can handle it."

Julietta looked over at her and smiled weakly. "Thanks, love. I still feel like I don't get it, though. I can understand why the 1% types are funding Sludge, or Fox or whatever. It's a bottom line thing for them: If we defend government that can only mean their taxes going up. But deep down I just don't get how easy it is for them to whip these hate squads up. Maybe it's all Trump's fault, although that seems too easy. But the raw fury ..." She trailed off but grabbed Ayala's hand that felt so at home resting on her thigh. "Anyway. I'm sorry for dragging you into it. And for going on about it."

Ayala said, "Hardly! We all made the decision for you to run together. I was on board then, and I still am. We all are. Felicia mentioned something else, about you not wanting to respond?"

Ayala felt Julietta's body re-wind and tense up. "Is that what this is about? Did Felicia conscript you into this?"

Ayala said, "No, no, no. Honest. But she did mention it. She seemed concerned but didn't say much beyond that." Julietta was still stony and silent. Ayala added, "Really."

Julietta said, "Felicia thinks we should drag the whole field staff into the muck and train them to respond to it, or even bring it up in the canvassing scripts. I think it's a terrible mistake ... I think it'd be the fastest way to blow it up even worse."

Ayala said, "Ah."

Julietta said, "I'm just so sick of talking about this and thinking about it. Yes, my family is weird. Yes, I like to fuck my friends. No, it's not anyone's damn business. And yes, we need to talk about anything other than this. My stock response when it comes up is 'Yes, you've read about my wonderful and different family on the internet, but we need to talk about how Americans are working harder for lower pay.' And I think that's basically working."

Ayala, "Well, I certainly see where you're coming from."

Julietta said, "I don't know if there's much else to say. I guess I need to talk to Felicia some more. Ugh." Ayala was wondering if she should have brought it up, but then Julietta said, "Maybe we shouldn't talk any more work stuff. Where the heck are we going, anyway?"

Ayala grinned, trying not to give away her secret but wondering if she had a tell. "Just for a hike! Up in Redwood."

They talked about the kids for the rest of the drive, parked, and headed up into the canyon. Ayala managed to casually guide them toward Doug's set up. When they got to the cairn, Ayala said, "What a sweet little cairn. I wonder what's up this path?"

Now Julietta was finally a bit suspicious, "What are you up to here?" But Ayala just smiled and took her hand and pulled her gently up the hill.

Unfortunately there was no old-growth forest in this part of the Bay. It had all been logged in the nineteenth century. But this must have been second growth; Doug had managed to find some of the tallest redwoods around and built the tiny camp there. The mattress was on the ground in the center of the ring and covered with a down comforter and a bunch of pillows, leaning up against one of the trees. The deep red cloth draped between the trees gave it almost a sense of it being an outside room or a little private temple. It was ethereally silent, the only noise being a slight rustle of leaves in the breeze far above them, sunlight filtering down and dappling the ground.

Julietta gasped. "You! And Doug, I'm guessing."

"Yup!"

"You two! Unreal." A worried look clouded her face. "I don't know what you have in mind here, but you know I'm running for Congress, right? We're not going to do anything that would make Felicia's life even more difficult or end up on another icky website, are we?"

Ayala got a slightly fiendish look. "We're in the middle of nowhere. Don't worry, we're not going to get caught." Then she took Julietta's hand over her protests as she mumbled something about being only a mile from a bunch of houses and led her over to next to the mattress and stood in front of her. Their eyes met and both of them looked down, with Ayala kissing her slowly, backing away a bit and running her hands over Julietta's shoulders and her chest and pausing at her heart for a few breaths, then moving her hands down along her sides to under her tank top. Ayala rested her hands on Julietta's hips and then dug her fingers under the waistband of her loose running shorts, lifted her shirt over her head, and ran her hands over the brown curves of Julietta's belly, under her bra, then lifting that over her head too. Julietta had been holding back, still worried. But as she felt the warm breeze on her exposed breasts, something shifted and let go. She pushed Ayala back until she was sitting on the mattress and stripped off her shorts herself, so she was standing naked in front of her. She stepped forward until Ayala's mouth was on her, kissing her legs and hair then slowly running her tongue down deeper into her and around her clit, moaning into her.

It didn't take long before Ayala's mouth was driving Julietta crazy. Julietta draped one leg over Ayala's shoulder and pulled her head in toward her. Ayala ran her hands up the muscles of the one leg holding her up, stabilizing her hips and pulling Julietta's sopping wet cunt towards her even harder. When Ayala grabbed her ass and pulled it towards her, Julietta came, loudly enough that they both got scared and laughed as she tumbled down onto the mattress.

"Oh love, thank you thank you thank you." Julietta snuggled up against Ayala, tasting herself as she kissed her. The turn on from her first orgasm had her hands moving down Ayala's shirt and under it, exploring every inch of her, then pulling her up a bit so she could slide her shirt and bra off too. Then her mouth was down on Ayala's

52

nipples, feeding off her, grabbing her chest with an edge of roughness and sucking them hard. Ayala moaned gutturally. Julietta pulled back after a bit and they locked eyes again, and Ayala could feel Julietta letting go of another layer of everything weighing on her. Julietta put her arm on her chest, pinning her to the mattress, and Ayala felt herself merging into the floor of the forest, merging into the trees and the wind and the light, merging into Julietta's swirling love and white hot desire for her. Ayala was moaning and grinding her crotch into Julietta's leg, so Julietta stuck her hand down the front of her shorts and started rubbing her clit, her hand following the unseen pathways it had followed so many time before.

Julietta gently put her fingers inside Ayala, then alternated between that and light touch over her clit again. Through waves of pleasure, Ayala touched Julietta back. They both slowed down, barely touching each other, their hands lightly running over each other's cunts. Breathing deeply, their energies wrapping around each other and now Julietta felt the merging sensation too. They were both lying there quietly, touching each other lightly but precisely, when another distant orgasm started building. They felt it cresting toward them and it hit them both at once, a shattering wave, like flying into a star. Ayala's legs and core muscles contracted and she squirted powerfully as Julietta cradled her, catching the brunt of the energy herself and having a ricochet wave of orgasmic intensity in return. Ayala rolled on top of her and fired another wave of orgasms back at her with her hands, finally collapsing next to her, as they held each other, lying still, reverberations of ecstasy still echoing through them for a long while.

They both floated in the wave of pleasure that had just hit them. As Julietta was starting to come down, her consciousness reforming and shaping itself back into reality, she started to sob. Long, drawn heavy breaths, wracking pain coming from deep inside her. Ayala held her and held her, opening to it, letting it all come through her too. She was grateful this emotional release was happening, even while she was angry at the sources generating it. Julietta passed into a wave of anger then too, cursing through the rage and shame and fear for her family, then tapping into a deeper fear for the future. She was afraid of being unable to end the cycle of oppression and sadness, of maybe not being able to budge it a little bit. She felt the pain of the fear; fear of not just getting things going in the right direction, but of even slowing down the decline of things at all.

She clung to Ayala as the anger passed and another wave of ecstatic pleasure reverberated into her from out of nowhere. She wailed, intertwining her legs and grinding back down on one of Ayala's thighs and coming again. Then finally collapsing and returning to their commingled, still synchronized breath.

"Whew. That. Wow. Where did that even come from." Julietta put her hand on Ayala's belly. "Can you imagine how good this kid must feel right now, with all that oxytocin in your bloodstream?"

Ayala was crying too. "It's true! The kid is going to be addicted to the stuff. Oh, love. They aren't going to beat you, I just know it. You are amazing."

Julietta started crying again, this time more gently. Ayala said, "What is it? It's more than the threats and the fear, isn't it."

When Julietta could talk she said quietly, "It's more than that. It's this ... gap that I've been thinking about. We have a good life. We don't have money and probably can't ever retire, but we have more security than most people. And we're lucky to get to do this, to join this fight. But the deeper I go into it, the more utterly intolerable injustice is. I'm thinking about where I was at when I was teaching, and then on that living wage campaign or the city council campaigns, and where I'm at now."

Ayala said, "I think there's a lot of power in that gap."

Julietta replied, "What do you mean?"

"Well, when I look at you and the past couple of years, I just think

... I don't know. Maybe I'm wrong. But I don't think you're going to ever give up. Not with the soul level commitment you've made."

Julietta said, "I don't know. I might give up. And even if I don't, it could all disappear tomorrow. Anything can happen. That's what these threats are about, right?"

Ayala said, "What else would you do?"

Julietta said, "Other than this?" She thought for a second, looking out at the trees and still sniffling. "I have no idea. Go back to teaching, maybe? Maybe we could get out of the Bay Area, get off the treadmill. But I just know I'd find more kids like the kids that persuaded me to get into that living-wage fight in the first place. Kids with parents with three jobs that still were struggling. That'd happen wherever we went."

She shrugged. "Plus, now I'm just whining. With the house and our community set up the way it is, the treadmill is a hell of a lot slower more under our control than it is for almost everyone else who lives here. What's Max's phrase for it?"

Ayala said, "'Community operationalizes decolonization from capitalism.' Something like that."

"Right. Plus if there was nothing else, I couldn't give up on Lauren. Do you remember the OPD rape scandal from a few years ago? Cops were literally trading protection to sex workers for sex. One of the women was her cousin. She told me about it a couple of years ago. I'd almost forgotten it was her, until the death threats started coming in and we were going to maybe call the cops."

Julietta felt Ayala's body tense up, like she'd been hit in the stomach. Ayala said, "Holy shit."

Julietta said, "Yeah. She's of course not the only reason I talk about police reform, and since I'm not openly in favor of completely defunding the police some of the groups aren't supporting me. OPD has gotten somewhat better over the past few years, but it's still completely out of control nationally, and I agree with them, we have to change the laws. Fixing that is never not going to be a priority for me." She sighed, looking around at the trees. "I guess you're right. I can't go back to teaching. Not now anyway. Powell's not going to fix that shit. Maybe Powell from years ago, but not now."

Ayala said, "OK, I know what you don't want. But what is that you do want?"

Julietta said, "So many things ..." and Ayala said, "Wait, I have an idea. Don't say anything about it. Just lie there and let go. Dream into it."

Julietta laughed gently at her. "Why? What for? You're weird."

Ayala shushed her and started running her hands over her body again. A slight breeze rustled over them and her skin lit up electrically. Ayala whispered again, quietly in her ear this time, "Let go, let go." She nibbled on her ear, running her tongue behind her earlobe.

Julietta said, "Damn, that feels good." Ayala whispered something in Hebrew to her.

Julietta was about to ask Ayala what it meant, but instead closed her eyes and lay back and gasped as she plunged into what felt like a entirely different reality. She was flying, moving across the California landscape, but it was all different. The big cities were still there, but they'd expanded upward and outward. Rail lines with fast trains connected a series of small cities. The cities were built on a similar repeating hexagonal pattern: a few tall buildings at the center, surrounded by tendrils of several story buildings and a few houses out in the country. Julietta plunged deeper into the vision and found it wonderfully detailed. She was able to see the functioning of the little cities, how nearly everything was walkable and bikeable, with parks and green space everywhere and small packs of kids running through them. Art was everywhere: huge murals and sculptures were scattered everywhere. Every neighborhood seemed to have landscaped pools, forests, and immaculate sports fields. The thought that it looked a bit like Disneyland flitted through her mind and she laughed a little. Ayala wondered what triggered the laugh but kept quiet.

She dropped into another structure she didn't recognize at first, but then realized it was a school. It was half open to the wilderness and half warehouse, with clusters of children working on projects, some of them reading, some of them playing games. Time sped up, and she went through a day. People woke up early but commuted slowly, and left their work and schools and labs earlier. The entire afternoon was consumed with cooking and eating, or reading and thinking and walking and daydreaming and playing, with groups of adults and kids gathering together and laughing into the night.

She came back to reality a bit, dimly aware of Ayala, who had moved down between her legs, kissing the outer surfaces of her lips so slowly and gently that it was nearly imperceptible. Julietta breathed in and said, "What the ..." and Ayala whispered "Let go, let go" and repeated the Hebrew phrase another time.

Julietta was consumed again. She felt the energy usage of the society coming from wind turbines and gleaming solar panels. She could sense the food systems, groups of people eating local food at long tables that had come from hundreds of small-scale organic operations around the little cities.

She found herself wondering how the economy worked, and a series of glowing, undulating green clouds of arrows appeared over the landscape and she realized it was vectors showing how money was flowing. It was clear that most of the wealth was under democratic control; large arrows flowed inward toward the government buildings in each community and then toward Sacramento, where she saw it being pumped back out into thousands of schools and universities and a dizzying amount of labs and small companies. She flew south and saw a spaceport emerging from the desert and looked up to a shimmering space station.

57

Then she pulled back down into the airspace of the state. Los Angeles was different, the highways were nearly empty, and it had been reformed into something not so different from the rails and small towns of farther north, with some long corridors of gorgeous, immense buildings. She could feel the diversity across all forms of identity: gender and sexual preferences and race and ethnicity and religion, and she could feel democracy and emotions pulsing through the whole system. Heartbreak and fear and hope and struggle and determination from the families to the workplaces and neighborhoods and cities, outward and upward.

Ayala had increased the intensity of kissing Julietta's pussy and Julietta was dimly aware of it, while still immersed in the vision. The vision started to brighten and fade into whiteness, and Julietta's entire consciousness was soon overtaken by the wonderful feelings radiating into her whole body from Ayala's mouth on her. Julietta gasped again as another wave of pleasure rose and then collapsed, and she fell into a rollicking, convulsing train of orgasms. As she started to emerge from them she was laughing and saying "Wow" over and over.

Ayala moved up next to her kissing her neck as Julietta's convulsions still shuddered through her body. After a bit Ayala said "Hi!" and Julietta laughed more. "You go somewhere interesting there?"

Julietta said, "Woah. You have no idea." She was panting still but starting to pull it together. "You really are a sorceress."

Ayala said, "What happened?"

Julietta said, "I just had a really clear, really detailed vision. I was flying, and the state looked different. Like, everything. It was like every conversation Doug and I have ever had about stuff, but compressed and turned real. I could feel how the money and food and energy flowed, even how the democracy worked, and people's emotions. That was nuts." She looked over at Ayala, radiating

58

appreciation from her eyes and her smile. "Thank you thank you thank you."

Ayala said, "You're certainly welcome. Have to say that's not what I was expecting to happen!"

Julietta said, "Yeah me neither! Well, this is sure going to make knocking on doors this afternoon feel like less of a chore, though." She sat up but wobbled a bit. Ayala steadied her, then sat up too. Julietta looked around and noticed the pitcher and poured two glasses of water, offering one to Ayala. She giggled a little. "Iced lemon cucumber water?"

"I'd be delighted!"

Julietta said, "Well, Doug sure earned himself a pile of karma today. I feel ready to fight again."

Ayala said, "I'm SO glad to hear that, love. Me too."

They clinked their glasses and touched each other and stayed suspended in their temporary escape nest for a few more minutes, as long as Julietta felt like she could get away with it.

6

That night, Julietta crawled into bed then reached over and turned off the light. Ayala preferred to sleep alone most nights, particularly now that she was pregnant, so Doug and Julietta shared a bed most of the time. Julietta lay on her back staring up at their bedroom ceiling. "Doug, did we blow it?"

Doug sighed, "Blow what, darling?"

Julietta said, "My campaign. It's possible we can't come back from this Sludge thing."

Doug yawned and went to roll over and said, "I'm so, so tired. You're going to be fine."

She grabbed him and prevented him from rolling over. "Come on. I'm serious."

Doug said, "No really, I'm not up for being blamed for this right now."

Julietta said, "What are you even talking about? I'm not blaming you!" He grunted skeptically. "Really."

Doug said, "Here's another theory. Shit happens. Politics is hard."

Julietta said, "Sure, but this feels a little like an unforced error. Like, great, I get to bonk my friends, but how much more suffering will there be if Powell wins."

"Maybe he won't be that bad." He sighed. "Plus, he's not going to win."

Julietta said, "Right." She paused. "But if he's not going to be that bad, why am I running? It sucks. I knew it would suck, but I hate it more than I thought I would."

Doug said, "There's a good chance he will be exactly that bad. We talked circles around this when he first got in. "

Julietta said, "Just think about anything he's running on. Like that 5% tax cut. That's how many fewer jobs the government would be able to fund in a crazy unemployment crisis? It's just all the way the wrong direction. That's a lot of pain."

"So OK, right. He's that bad."

Julietta said, "So why are we prioritizing me bonking my friends over my career again?"

Doug said, "We didn't know this would happen! It's not like when we met Ayala we could have predicted anything like this. If this is a failure, it's a pretty complicated cascading set of decisions that led to it. It's not any one thing."

Doug wasn't sure if their path to nonmonogamy was weird, or a not-so-unusual path to a somewhat unusual destination. He'd first tried it almost a decade before meeting Julietta. A friend had handed him a copy of The Ethical Slut, the first book to lay out the basic principles of ethical nonmonogamy in an approachable way, after a discussion over brunch of how frustrating dating was. Doug flipped through it and saw a chapter titled "You are already whole." That was all it took to convince him to give it a read.

He'd always assumed that he'd give it up and settle down at some point; shuffling "open to nonmonogamy" into all the other things he sought in a partner seemed impossible. But when he mentioned it to Julietta on one of their early dates, she surprised him later by asking about it more, and eventually they talked their way into giving it a try by going on a few dates with another couple they knew. They'd tiptoed into it, a bit at a time, and managed to never give up on it despite challenges over the years. So, by the time they met Ayala they were both solid in their openness to her in a way that Ayala found irresistible, despite it not being something she'd ever seriously considered either.

Julietta said, "So yeah. Not mistakes. Just decisions with unforeseen consequences."

Doug said, "It does raise the question, though: Why were you even interested in being like this? I don't know that I've ever even asked you that."

Julietta said, "I'm not sure I even know. I mean, some of it must be from my family. Since my parents split up when I was little, it's not like anyone was drilling into me how great monogamy was."

Doug grunted a laugh, and said, "You know we can't exactly quit."

Julietta said, "Yeah, I know. Obviously. And I like how things are with us, of course. I love Ayala, and Max, and Ananda too. And I'm completely freaking out about all of us having a new baby. Freaking out in a good way. It seems so right."

Doug said, "So, we are bell hooks' revolutionary parenting, we're living it. There's another thing, though, something I've been thinking about. Would you have run without our life being the way it is?"

Julietta said, "That's a good question."

Doug said, "I think maybe no. Without things being so relatively stable for us, why would you bother? Not that they're even all that stable, really, but we've certainly got it easier than most everyone we know. If we lived alone, had a kid or two, were juggling things constantly, always being too tired for sex, with both of us working full time, or even if I just worked and we weren't sharing childcare—just on a practical level, I'm not sure how you would have swung it. Even if we had more money."

Julietta said, "I probably wouldn't have had either the motivation or the ability."

Doug nodded. "Right. The better stuff is, the more wrong it seems to not to fight for it for everyone."

"Yeah. I just have no idea if running for congress is the right way to do that though."

Doug said, "I don't either. But what else can we do? You saw an open shot and you're taking it." A wave of exhaustion hit him at the same moment as a sense this conversation was going to be hard to end. He rolled back up next to her and slowly ran his hands under the little shorts she was wearing. As he expected from how she'd described her day, her cunt was still sopping wet. He started touching her but then his touch slowed, and soon she noticed he was snoring softly. She laughed a little. Her mind drifted off the campaign and back to Ayala's touch and the warmth of the vision she'd had, and she fell asleep feeling somewhat reassured.

The response to the campaign after the Sludge Report pictures was split in half. In the district and inside the campaign, it felt like nothing much had changed. Hardly any of the voters they were contacting had heard anything about it beyond the initial small bump that Felicia had picked up, so they continued to hold off on responding publicly.

But online, they were under a complete onslaught. The servers from all their online tools had been hit with "denial of service" attacks repeatedly. One day Julietta came in to find two of the online ops folks asleep under their desks. She brought them flowers that afternoon.

They were getting an appalling amount of comments in response to anything they posted anywhere online. Cruel jabs, antisemitism, disgusting pictures and rape jokes at first, and then it escalated more toward threats on Doug and her, and then, astonishingly, veiled threats directed at their kids. They were fired off at every Twitter account related to the campaign, and then another wave of tweets that were directed at anyone who had mentioned Julietta's campaign positively. Ayala, Fruity First, and their old friend Kiyana from the pictures had abuse coming at them from seemingly out of nowhere.

They couldn't tell if it was well-organized or just network-amplified, Trump-inspired emergent chaos, but it was targeting their entire little constellation of lovers, friends, and family members. They'd seen responses like this for years aimed at smart, aggressive women who had put themselves out there as advocates. Seeing it from a distance didn't prepare them for the true awfulness of how it felt in the moment.

They'd gotten some amount of support from a couple of different anti-abuse organizations, which helped them cope with it but didn't seem to visibly slow or have any affect on the attacks. At the suggestion of one of their contacts there, they skipped talking to the police and went straight to the FBI. The federal cops couldn't do much, but they could at least keep track of it and plug what they were reporting into existing investigations of online abuse. But it was all so limited. When one of the waves of attacks from a bunch of new accounts flooded Ayala's Twitter account with a cartoon of her and Avi being thrown into ovens, she went to email the reports to the FBI and found the same images there. She burst into tears after slamming her laptop shut.

Unfortunately the death threats were only the beginning. The campaign had spent a lot of energy on aggressive outreach to local news sources. News organization endorsements had been on the decline in strategic relevance for decades, particularly among the younger and mostly disengaged new voters they were trying to reach, but they'd recently had something of a resurgence after the proliferation of endorsement-based voting apps and websites, where voters could quickly pull up and compare endorsements from any organizations. Increasing numbers of voters were ignoring useless TV and online ads and starting to use these new tools to make decisions in local elections, particularly during primaries.

All but six of the twenty-five Bay Area news sources they'd reached out to endorsed Powell. Disturbingly, all but two of those endorsements of her opponent included at least some kind of vague or veiled mention of her family structure. They didn't go directly for it; it was all coded and strange, with weird, awkwardly structured, view-from-nowhere arguments that praised her economic vision but stopped short of supporting her. The closest they got to making an argument for Powell was that he'd work better with conservatives, even though they (often in the same endorsement!) vigorously opposed the ideas the Republicans were fighting for.

Doug was enraged. "Chalk another one up for team hetero white dude. We are this far into the 21st century and this is still happening! What is the point of compromising on a bunch of a shitty ideas? This is bullshit."

Soon after the wave of endorsement-related bad news, and just before ballots were hitting the electorate's mailboxes, they started to really feel the effect of the Sludge Report on the field campaign side. Where it had been quiet before now it started to show up everywhere, from what voters were saying on the phone and in replies to their texts, to lower attendance at public events to the local meetings with their neighborhood teams. Julietta sat in on a text messaging bank, mostly to buck up the volunteers but also to see what people were saying first hand. The replies were depressing but not surprising: "It just seems like she'd be distracted … I suppose it's good for her, although I would never let my husband do such a thing," and of course the occasional, "Oh, she's cute, I'm glad she has my phone number!" Blogs and social media alone couldn't drive the story, but once the corporate media started to hint at it, even vaguely, it closed the communications loop and increased the rate that her personal life was defining the campaign.

When the results came in of the focus group they ran on their core base of unmarried women, what they discovered confounded them totally. Their base wasn't switching to Powell. The more he tacked to the center and gained institutional support, the more voters were annoyed and turned off by him. What the voters were doing then was tuning out completely. The underlying emotions they picked up on were disgust and even a little bit of raw fear. It was as if the attacks on Julietta had been aimed directly at the gag reflex of her base. Her voters still identified with her, but that made the attack work even better. It made it that much harder for people to watch what was being done to her.

Wherever the attacks on Julietta were coming from, they were either very lucky, or very, very sophisticated.

Things seemed to be holding tough through the last several days. Julietta, after weeks of pressure, finally gave Felicia permission to muster the neighborhood leadership to fight back, and that seemed to more or less work without blowing the issue up any larger than it already was. Anytime the family subject came up in a conversation at someone's door or in a neighborhood meeting, her volunteers and staff were on message. As far as they could tell from the responses pouring in from the field campaign, they'd certainly taken a hit among supporters and those who were still undecided on voting, but it wasn't for sure going to sink them.

Then with just three weeks to go before Election Day, the campaign got a medium-sized Fed-Ex box with "District 12 Alliance" on the return address. Felicia opened it, dumped out a bunch of printed research reports, and rolled her eyes. "Printouts!" But she fed them out to the policy team and asked them to sort it all out.

After the staff had left to knock on doors the next day, Felicia stuck her head into Julietta's office, dropping the pile of research papers down on her desk with a soft thud. "So, as you know, D12 sent us a bunch of stuff. I had our policy people go over it last night."

Julietta said, "And?"

"Well, to be totally honest, most of it is way off target. There's a few items, which they helpfully highlighted, suggesting voters aren't ready to hear about reparations or public investment or some of the other things we're talking about."

Julietta interrupted, "And let me guess: nothing substantive, nothing about how to actually fix the problems or make things better and nothing about what voters are ready to hear, or how to move them?"

Felicia shrugged, "A few things. They sent a letter summarizing what they thought would work. Job training programs was most of it."

Julietta was pissed now. "What the hell. Training for WHAT jobs?"

Felicia was placid. "Yep. So, we can ignore this, right?"

"What else did the letter say?"

Felicia replied, "It was a bit ominous. I don't know if this is good news or not, but they invited you to come to their conference, two weeks after the campaign."

Julietta said, "Oh, that's actually probably a good thing."

Felicia hesitated and then said, "Really? Even if ..." She caught herself before saying "you lose," and added, "things don't go well?"

"Well if that happens, that happens." She stared at Felicia, irritated. "At least it'll be a chance for me to present our side of the story. But in the meantime this stuff is useless." She gestured at the pile of research. "Fuck. Felicia, maybe we should back off more. Pivot a little here. There is just too much stuff coming at us. Sludge, the threats, now this. I really can't wait for this thing to be over. I miss my kids."

Felicia said, "I'm sure you do, but we have to finish this. I say we fire back. Let's go negative on him. We haven't until now. No reason not to. We already cut the ads."

Julietta was getting more irritated. "Those ads suck. I'm sorry.

They're not going to work. We even said this when we made them. Nothing is working."

Felicia shrugged again, "OK then let me make new ads."

Julietta stared. "With WHAT BUDGET?"

"Remember those filmmakers who approached us about making an ad? We could talk to them. Their work was good."

"Felicia. Their crowdfunding videos were lovely, but they'd never done a political ad in their life. Everything they suggested was ridiculous."

"Those were just their first ideas! They were smart, I'm sure we could come up with something better. Get Lauren and Henry involved."

Julietta stood up. "We're not fucking going negative on Powell. I'm not sure we could if we wanted to, beyond what we've been saying anyway. His ideas are shitty and won't work, and mine are better. I'm going to keep saying that. It's either going to work or it isn't."

Felicia looked at her. "You're giving up, aren't you."

Julietta lost it. "For fucks sake. NO. I am NOT giving up. I just don't want to waste our time on something that we can't afford and that wouldn't work if we could afford it. Seriously Felicia. Drop it. I'm going to go knock on some fucking doors."

Felicia said, "Their bullshit attacks actually worked. Great. Yeah, go knock on some doors. That'll work. Fucking hell."

Felicia got up, picked up the pile of papers, and stalked out, slamming the office door behind her. The rest of the office was deserted, and she took the entire stack and hurled the whole thing towards the far wall. It never got there, exploding in a satisfying mess all over the floor.

Julietta walked out of her office with her backpack and purse, took one look at the mess, snorted derisively, and left.

She trudged through the last couple weeks. She kept going; she owed it to her staff. Her speeches weren't awful, they were still definitely reaching people. But something was missing.

Then on the last weekend, the Powell campaign apparently decided to go for the kill. Both campaigns had stayed positive until now, not too unusual for a primary. Then Powell put up a contrast TV ad in what looked like a big buy on the Friday night before Election Day, across network and cable. It was just on TV, not a trace of it anywhere on his social media or online, so it was clearly aimed at the older part of the electorate. It wasn't horrifying or obviously divisive, but it ended with a shot of Powell, his traditionally attractive wife, and their two kids. In the context of this campaign it was like a dog-whistle for beige normalcy. The image of their more traditional-appearing family seared Julietta with doubt about a lot more than her campaign, and then anger about that doubt.

7

"Fuuuuuuuuuuuuuuck. I fucking, fucking hate fucking losing." Julietta moaned, lying face up on the brown carpeted floor, her head in Ayala's lap and Max rubbing her feet, all of them sprawled in front of a picture window view of the lights of Oakland in the foreground and San Francisco on the other side of Treasure Island, flickering hopefully from the cool, breezy night. The view from the large hotel suite they'd rented for Election Night was exceptionally lovely, and the dozen or so activists and campaign staff in the suite were all completely ignoring it. Alexander, Elijah, and Avi were playing games in the bedroom while Nora crawled around between the various grownups.

Julietta looked out the window and wanted to cross the bay and go and get lost in the bigger city. Just disappear, dissolve into seedy dive bars, maybe wind up at a strip joint or a sweaty dance club or underground party, leave the kids with her parents and take Doug and Max and Ananda and Ayala and they could all lose themselves. The feeling passed quickly, and she resumed facing the ugly reality of her loss.

"Darling, I'm pretty sure you haven't had nearly enough to drink."

Doug leaned back in his chair, checking her out in spite of the ambient foul mood of the room. Black knee-high boots in a pile next to her. Patterned tights, her favorite black skirt, wine-red tight blouse, almost a corset, with a lacy black bra just visible underneath. Her coat with the subtle lace-up sides—just a hint of domme, somehow the laces transmitted power—

hung on the chair next to her. She said, "I'm not sure that's true! I think I have to give a speech later."

He poured another gin and tonic and held it near the floor for her, just in reach. Julietta propped herself up on her elbows just enough to grab the drink and tip it into her mouth. "I told them this was a bad idea!" She imitated her friends, the allies, and donors and loves of hers who had talked her into this. "'It's practically an open seat, this area loves you, just show up in the primary and see where it goes, don't worry that you're running against your old friend, imagine being in Congress from the district next to Barbara Lee, sure you have a new one year old and another little kid but you have an amazing husband and your kids will understand!' they said. Blah blah blah. Fuck."

Doug said, "Ouch. Well, the amazing husband part is right at least." She looked up at him and laughed. "You did this to me!" She looked serious for a minute. "No really, you did. Right when we met, when you told me about being nonmongamous. It sounded fun!" Doug said, "We already had this fight. You could have said no thanks! But you're really cut out for it." Julietta laughed. "Putting that particular toothpase back in that particular tube wasn't going to happen." She looked around at Max, Ananda, and Ayala. "Thank you all for being here with me."

Max said, "Doug shouldn't get all the blame here. Maybe it's my fault. We keep shoveling personal economic security from the kibbutz at you two, and you just keep trying harder stuff."

Julietta laughed but said, "You may have a point." She looked at

Doug, "You're partially off the hook then, love." Doug looked mock-relieved. A cell phone rang, and Felicia picked it up, said, "OK" and hung up and said, "Julietta, it's time."

Julietta said, "Oh shit, the concession. Right." She looked around the room. "I might be still in too much of a fighting mood for this." She stood up, leaned over to smooch Ayala, and then swayed a little and made some air punches. "We have the speeches Felicia and I wrote, but anyone have any last minute ideas?" Everyone stared at their drinks as the noise from the TV Election Night coverage crackled in the background.

Max finally broke the silence. "Don't let the bastard off the hook. I think you can do this without being graceless. What he did was not OK. He might have been at best a frenemy lately, but he used to be an ally. We know where he was coming from. He knew better than to pull this crap." Max was convinced Powell was behind both the D12 and Sludge attacks. Murmurings of what seemed like agreement came from around the room, but Julietta wasn't convinced. Max might be leading with too hot of a response, which was usually Doug's department.

"Felicia, that seem OK to you?"

Felicia paused, thinking it through. "I think you can mention the slut-shaming thing even though we have no idea it came from him. Just don't go too crazy with it, don't attempt to tie it to him." She looked over at Max and mouthed "Sorry." Max rolled his eyes.

Julietta said, partially to Max and more to herself, "We still don't know where these attacks came from. Not really. Even if we think we kind of know. The worst part is, he definitely backed away from what he used to believe in. I can call him out on that, right? Subtly?"

Felicia said, "Look: you lost, it sucks right now, and we're still numb. It's going to hurt a whole bunch worse in the morning." Julietta and Doug both groaned at this, recognizing the truth of it instantly from past experience. "But you stayed true to your core principles and we know for a fact Powell didn't. So, there's a high road path you can take here. Oh Lordy, protect us first from our allies."

Julietta said, "Speaking of the high road, I have to call him first, don't I." Doug tossed her cellphone down to her. She caught it and sat up. Nora had been crawling on her and whined so Doug snatched her up into her arms and gave her a tickle, eliciting a stream of giggles. Julietta stared at the phone in her hand for a minute, like she'd been suddenly handed a full diaper. But she dialed and soon it was ringing.

"Hiya, Steve."

"Hi there."

"Well, it's the call you've been waiting for." She paused for a second, not trying to be dramatic, just gathering herself. Hearing his voice on the other end of the line she was reminded of their connection and their history and she managed to eke out a little sincerity. "Congratulations, Steve. I'm not crazy about everything that happened, but you ran a good race."

"Thanks Julietta. Been a long trip since those conversations out in the desert, hasn't it." Apparently he was thinking the same thing, but Julietta was a little surprised he mentioned it. She was aware of the difference in their approaches since that time and thought again, He thinks what he did is just what you have to do.

"It sure has." An idea popped into her head, and before she could evaluate whether it was a good idea or a terrible one, she said, "Look, I know this is weird, but we're thinking about wrapping our party up early and coming to see you guys. After my speech." She knew they were holed up at Radium, a loft they'd all been to some legendary parties at together over the years. It was just a few blocks away, but now that it had tumbled out of her mouth she had no idea where the idea had come from. Doug, Max, Felicia, and Ananda all stared at her like she'd sprouted a third arm. Steve seemed to have no idea what to say. "Hunh! Well, OK. If you're not kidding, let's make this a real party. Any chance Doug would be up for djing a spot later?"

"Ha! Sure, let me ask him." She covered the phone and said to Doug, "He wants you to spin."

Doug laughed. "Just like old times, eh! OK. I'm in."

Julietta talked back into the phone. "He's down. I have to go say something to my people first, but I'll invite them too. It'd be good for local party unity and all that."

Steve said, "OK, great. I'll warn my crowd too. Julietta," he paused for a second. "Thanks for this. I'm still sorry about the Sludge Report crap, as you know."

She fended off from what she wanted to say, thinking of his last TV ad. "Well, it's a complicated business, right? We'll see you soon."

"Great, see you later." She hung up and stared at the phone and laughed at herself. Doug said, "You are a real piece of work, Former Congresswoman To Be Julietta Torres. The genuine freakin' deal." She looked up at everyone. "Come on, it's a primary. Thank mercy California dropped top twos and now we don't have run against him again." She was referring to the top two primary system that California briefly had used, which had weakened local parties and made general elections often wasteful rematches of primaries. Voters had finally gotten rid of it in one of the first true grassroots campaigns of the post-Trump surge of interest in democracy in the state. "Who knows what happens next. We know half the folks there, plus it'll be interesting to see who all shows up."

Max said, "I think she's right. Ananda? Felicia?"

Ananda said, "This whole thing is crazy and you people are crazy, and here I am with you. So I'm up for whatever."

Julietta grinned at her as Alexander, Avi, and Elijah came over. Elijah sat down in the crook of her arm and asked, "So, you lost, Mom?"

Julietta said, "Yeah, I did. But, it's OK because sometimes losing teaches you more than winning. And you can't give up. Not ever."

Elijah said, "I get it. We get to go be on stage now, right?"

Julietta smiled and said, "Yep, let's do it!" Julietta put her arms around Ananda and Max and said, "One last question. All of us on stage, or just Doug, Elijah, and me?" She looked around at them. "I know what I want," she didn't need to add "all of us," but her voice shook a little as she said, "but I've dragged you all down deep into this thing so far already, maybe we should just let it all be over."

A collective gush went out from all of them. Doug watched Max and Ananda looking at each other and nod. Ananda said, "Sweetie, we started out making this decision as a team. We're in. It'd be an honor."

Ayala reached over and stroked Julietta's cheek. "Me too. So there for you."

Julietta smiled and wiped at a tear and said, "I really love you people. I'm sorry we didn't pull it off. But I am incredibly lucky to be so supported by all of you." They packed up the kids and filed out, the staff trailing behind them. As they got in the elevator, the five of them stood along the back wall, all holding hands. Julietta was on the end and reached forward to grab Felicia's hand, too. Stepping off the elevator they headed into the hotel's large ballroom. It was packed and bustling—there was a particular ambient conversational intensity that only a room with a few hundred political activists could generate —but a rain cloud definitely hung over the crowd. It was dimly lit, with most of the light coming from spotlights aimed at Kiyana's art hanging from every corner, including the elaborately detailed, gorgeous ten-foot-high butterfly print she'd made for the original announcement. She'd surprised Julietta with it as a gift earlier in the evening, right after the polls closed, which had caused Julietta to burst suddenly into sobbing tears of gratitude for a few minutes. Her breath caught in her throat again when she saw it here.

A ripple of recognition, a swell of applause, and a crest of wild cheering went through the crowd as the five adults and three kids walked toward the stage. Julietta exchanged a look with the DJ, one of their favorites from Fruity First, who gave her a sad nod and grateful smile. Doug picked up Elijah and Avi, grateful they were just old enough to be grinning and not terrified of the racket. The applause settled but it still took them nearly fifteen minutes to hug their way through the outpouring of affection to reach the stage. As Julietta climbed up toward the microphone with her family constellation next to her the crowd swelled again, wilder this time. She tried to calm it and then gave up, then finally it started to settle enough for her to be heard and she said, "Thank you, thank you, thank you." She took a deep breath, looked down at her notes on the podium, set them aside, pulled the microphone out of the stand, and approached the front of the stage.

8

"Hi, everyone. Thank you. This has been an amazing thing to be a part of. So grateful to be here, and I'm incredibly grateful for all of you. Grateful from the bottom of my soul. You all have built something incredible. It didn't start with this campaign, and it is not going to end tonight. However, it's true that we are not here to celebrate a victory tonight." An anguished wail went up, and she waited again. "It's OK, it's OK. I know. But we are here to celebrate what we've built and renewing our ongoing commitment to the great project of American democracy." The applause rose again, quieter.

"Of course I support Steve Powell going into the general election. I expect you all to, too. Let's take what we built here and help him with it. Then he'll have to listen to us!" More cheers. "Seriously, he's going to be a great representative, and we are lucky to have him. In fact I talked to him earlier this evening. Their party is down the street at Radium and we are all invited down there. We're going to stick around here for a bit," she gestured at Doug, Ananda and Ayala, and the kids, "but in an hour or so head over. I hope you'll join us. And I know a lot of you hoped this would happen tonight but Doug will be DJing over there later." This yielded whoops from a few folks in the crowd and a smattering of applause that seemed sort of puzzled.

"But while I've got you here ..." she waited for a second, looking out at all of them. "As you all know, this campaign was about the future of the American family and the future of how we work. And really, it is about our vision of freedom. Our real opponents—and I don't mean Steve Powell here, I mean the people who attacked my family during this campaign." The crowd booed loudly. "Let me tell you what is going on with this. They think freedom is mostly about keeping taxes low on rich folks and having lots of stuff. And if that means you have to work sixty or eighty hours a week and get fired at any time, or not have a job at all, that's tough. I'm being a bit harsh here, but they really do think that not having any rules about work is the best way for you to have security. It's not that they don't care about your freedom. They think they do. They just have the wrong ideas about what freedom really is. We've tried their ideas, and they aren't working."

"So, we ran on a new vision. A real role for government, and government that works for everyone, not just the wealthy. We laid out our vision for a person-oriented society as best we could. That's true freedom: a society that cares deeply about people and their unlimited potential, and one that shapes its institutions around those values. Some of you got very excited about that, and so did a lot of the voters in our district. Just not enough of them!" People laughed a bit, and Julietta felt like some of the rain clouds started to break up. "We have a lot of work to do still.

"We support each other and we want justice. These are our shared values. And we have so many shared objectives: We're going to build a country that works for more than the 1%. We're going to make college free again, like it used to be in this state under the great expansionary plans of the sixties. We're going to accelerate the great work on renewable energy systems that our state has already invested in. We're going to get rid of traffic and congestion and build cities that work! Just imagine living without traffic. And we're going to address violence in all its forms, from gun culture to military spending to police accountability to ending mass incarceration.

"But we can't do it without all of us together. Sometimes people who run in other parts of the country say, we don't need to talk about race, we don't need to talk about diversity in this age of Trump, about what they call identity politics. But I'm sorry: All politics is identity politics, whether we want it to be or not. And because we can imagine this future where difference is respected and loved, we're not going to quit building it, even despite all the bumps in the road we keep hitting. How we treat those of us who are different, that's the core of our moral vision. There's a deep vision there that goes far beyond this surface fear of 'political correctness.' That deep vision spans all moral systems and all true religions. I'm not going to stop working on that, and I know you aren't either.

"So, I don't have much of a conclusion for you tonight, because the greater fight to build that world isn't over. It does not end tonight. I love you all, keep the faith, and let's keep fighting for a better vision for this country!"

Julietta stepped back, and as the applause swelled, they all looked at each other, putting their arms around each other. Doug, with a kid hoisted in either arm, gave her a smooch, then Max did, but she and Ayala and Ananda just smiled at each other, enjoying the temptation to kiss more than briefly too, while the crowd started to calm down and shortly returned to procuring and consuming beverages.

Things weren't really slowing down an hour later. Julietta had been out talking to the crowd, and the level of energy of the party amazed her. Everyone was still excited, plotting directions they could go to influence the Powell campaign and beyond. Of all the victory (and loss) parties they'd been to over the years, this one felt different. More like the speed bump than the crash into the bleak brick wall. She almost felt bad for Powell: He didn't need this pack of rabidly engaged voters to win in November, but they were going to make his life in office awfully unpleasant and brief if he didn't figure out how to reconcile them with his more tepid and centrist influences.

Julietta noticed Doug looking at her. "What?"

He said, "I'm just feeling the awe. You did something kind of amazing here. Look at this."

Julietta said, "I know! Wild times, love. Thank you so much for your help." They kept looking at each other, both vaguely aware there were lots of eyes on them but in their own created space and loving the feeling of their relationship being a little on display. In their forties now, they had a community of friends and loves filled with a lot of relationships that hadn't worked out, with a big uptick in separations and divorces in the last couple of years. But theirs somehow just kept going.

They ended up sneaking out of their own victory party, after Felicia offered to stay a bit longer and remind everyone to head over if they wanted to hear Doug's set. Ananda had gone far over her usual amount of social engagement for the week and took the kids home. Max, Doug, Ayala, and Julietta went out of the hotel the back way and made their way through the cool Oakland night to the loft, a few blocks away, slipping initially unrecognized into the back of Powell's party. Julietta couldn't help but notice the crowd looked to be about a third the size of hers.

They heard the loud thud of the bass, and there were a few people dancing upstairs, but the largest crowd was downstairs by the entrance and crowded around the monitors that were set up for election results. Julietta poked Doug in the ribs, "Woah, there's a whole election going on, I completely forgot!" She picked up her phone: 140 new text messages. She showed it to Doug, "Guess we are having a busy night."

They joined the back of the pack crowding the monitor, still unnoticed, and Doug checked his electoral dashboard app. "Oh boy, love. It's looking ugly."

Years before, Julietta had been one of the initial architects of the first Reflective Democracy initiative. It was a big, sprawling project aimed at attacking all the structural barriers preventing elected leadership from reflecting the true diversity of American communities. The three big barriers they'd identified had to do with money, what they called gatekeeper networks of organizations and consultants, and then the various structural ways that incumbents managed to abuse the system to protect themselves, mainly through gerrymandering and other sorts of crooked redistricting schemes.

It had taken years for this strategy to play out, after dozens of various pilot projects and experiments. This primary was one of the first times they had a substantive electoral cadre trying to move up through the system. They were tracking candidates at every level, municipal to state to federal. It was bipartisan; they'd had a much easier time recruiting Democrats but they did have a core group of dedicated centrist and even progressive Republican women running too. What these GOP women lacked in numbers they made up for in guts: They were challenging years of party orthodoxy and were reviled by the old guard, particularly once their messages started resonating with voters. Julietta had helped hire some brilliant staff to run the effort and stepped away from the project to run her own campaign, but of course she had still been tracking it closely.

The big challenge they faced was still depressed voter turnout in midterm elections. They'd first noticed the problem years ago: 42 million fewer voters voted in 2010 than 2008, and from 2012 to 2014 it got even worse, with 47 million fewer showing up. And in the primaries of course it was far worse. The difference was almost entirely among the young and racially diverse voters that Reflective Democracy campaigns, including Julietta's, needed to win. Some of the experiments they'd run in fixing this issue were getting positive results, but persuading national organizations run from DC to adopt their tactics was slow going.

Doug scrolled down through the app, and graphs and numbers flitted by. "Federal is a bloodbath, 24% so far. State 34 percent, municipal 43. Agggggggh. Still a bunch of races that haven't been called, though." He flicked through more pages. "OK; here's some good news: Remember how we had 56 candidates spread out around LA? Of the 37 we have results for, so far 31 are ahead." He scrolled a little more, "Although some not by much." He put his phone away and looked at up her. "Wow."

Julietta said, "Woah. I need to sit down. Now. Doug, love, I may need another drink." She looked around, "I'm going to get one myself, the bar's right over there." Doug had compulsively pulled his phone back out and was flipping through it again, but he mumbled "OK."

She got in line, briefly feeling a little indignity at having to wait in line for a drink at her opponent's party, and hoping someone would recognize her. Her wish was granted a second later when the woman in front of her glanced up from her phone and did a double take. She stuck out her hand and said, "So, you're Julietta Torres."

Julietta shook it and said, "Hi. Thank you for recognizing me, it's a little weird being here."

She said, "I bet. Erykah Williams, nice to meet you. Can I buy you a drink? Because wow did you ever fuck that campaign of yours up something terrible. You must need one."

Julietta's mind swept from pleasant campaign mode to knives and death rage mode instantly, but just smiled. "Well, a pleasure meeting you too, Ms. Williams. Have a terrific evening."

She turned to go and Erykah said, "Wait, wait, I'm sorry. Terrible habit I have. For an expert in communications I can be awful at communicating sometimes."

Julietta stopped and looked at her. She was tall, dark black skin, neat rows of tight braids casually pulled up, great smile, dressed stylishly. Could have been a corporate lawyer, maybe sales. Erykah said, "Came from my family growing up. My momma took no shit. I inherited many fine qualities from her too. Honest."

Julietta laughed at that. "You sure make an interesting first impression. What kind of communications?"

Erykah said, "Deep strategy. Went to Wharton, then a doctorate in neurolingustics from Berkeley. Mostly I do corporate stuff. I'm your basic worst nightmare when it comes to marketing and manipulation. But I've been getting a little more interested in politics lately."

Julietta took all this in and nodded. They got to the front of the line and both simultaneously ordered vodka and sodas, causing them both to crack up. Julietta said, "So, you can hydrate and drink at the same time, right?" Erykah laughed and nodded.

They got their drinks and stepped back over toward the clump of people watching the election results on the TV. Julietta traded a glimpse with Doug, and he raised an eyebrow at her. She could tell he thought she was on the make, but she turned back to Erykah and said, "I'm almost afraid to ask, but since we've already gone there, tell me, what'd I do wrong?"

She said, "Well, your framing was generally pretty good. Unlike most of the crap I hear from our side it was clear that you'd thought it through pretty well."

Julietta said, "Thanks. We did. A lot of it was the team; I have some good people. But it came from the top, too. I don't think it matters the way the substance matters." She couldn't resist adding, "or as much as the way some of the advocates of messaging think it does. But I do think it matters." She still wasn't sure where Erykah was coming from. Had she worked with Powell? So, she didn't want to say much.

Erykah said, "Well, that's the first step. The things that jumped out at me from the research we've been doing were pretty small details. Probably too much to get into now. There were some things around respect, and some values and aspiration language that you could have led with that would have increased your effectiveness. And some contrasts ..."

Julietta said, "We looked into some lines of contrast but found that it turned off a lot of our persuadables." Julietta was testing her with a little jargon. She wondered if Erykah understood fundamentals of campaigns, the process of identifying groups of voters that weren't with her initially but could be persuaded.

Erykah said, "Yeah, there's some steps you need to do in setting up your base and persuadable universes that you might not have done." There was her answer. She sure did. If she hadn't worked with Powell she'd certainly been around some other campaigns. "Anyway, too much in the weeds to get into at a party. We should talk more." She smoothly produced a card out of her purse. "Good luck, Julietta, a pleasure meeting you."

Julietta took the card and said, "First time in weeks I haven't had mine on me, but they're not much good at this point anyway except as collector's items. But nice meeting you too." Erykah smiled at her and left, and Julietta watched her go, with only a faint eye roll.

She went back and joined Doug, who said, "Well, that looked interesting. Flirting?"

Julietta said, "Ugh, no. Some corporate marketing person. Sort of interesting but too confident. Abrasive, maybe even icky."

He said, "Oh, bummer. You ready to go? I really don't much feel like playing, I'm sure I can flake."

"No, no; let's stick around a little longer, I just need to think all this through. But I should really call the Reflective Democracy folks and check in. They are going to be hurting."

She started dialing and went outside as Max, Ayala, and Doug wandered toward a couch at the other end of the basement, conveniently far away from the monitors. The four of them sat down in a depressed heap.

Which was how Powell found them when he came over. Doug stood up, "Hey, Steve. Congratulations, but the fight sure still goes on tonight, doesn't it?"

Powell looked serious and with a noticeable amount of genuine compassion said, "Sorry it didn't work out for you guys. Where's Julietta? I really do want to talk to her." She'd seen him come over and wrapped up her call and walked up at that moment, and they hugged. Doug's mood was still flat from the news from the wider campaign, but he did appreciate the momentary sweetness between Julietta and Powell. The two of them had started out in such a similar place, out in the desert watching the sun rise over a synthetic, temporary city, talking endlessly about where the future could go, but had taken such different paths since then. Even so, and even after being locked into democratic combat for the past year of campaigning, they could still easily share a connection.

Powell said, "I'm really glad you guys came. Doug, you still up for playing?"

Doug looked over at Julietta and could tell her answer was probably going to be a no. "Ahh, let's caucus for a bit and we'll let you know. We just got some bad news about the Reflective Democracy numbers."

"Oh, no. I'm sorry about this; you guys really did run a great campaign and it was an honor to run against you. I hope you'll stick around but I entirely understand and I do appreciate you coming by at least."

After he left they sat on the couch staring straight ahead again for a bit. Julietta started, "Babe, I am just not sure I'm up for this ..." when there was a bit of a commotion by the door.

The crowd of people around the TVs broke up and reformed around whomever had just walked in. Julietta looked sideways at Doug, and he shrugged. In a bit the crowd parted and they saw, but did not believe, who it was. Julietta looked over at them, "It looks like

..."

Doug finished, "Peter Dixon?"

"It makes sense ..." Julietta said, "Oh, it so does make sense. Oh, wow." A rush of thoughts hit her, remembering their old libertarian campmate from Burning Man and the endless arguments they'd had, and how Powell had always been a little squishy on refuting them. She'd never known if he was genuinely persuaded or just trying to keep the peace. "Could he have been behind ...?"

Doug finished her thought again. "The attacks? Oh, for fuck's sake." Thinking some, "We don't know anything, though. Can't rush to conclusions."

Julietta said, "OK, we are definitely not sticking around now."

They hoped Dixon and his posse would pass them by and head upstairs, but no such luck. He strode right over to them. Disarming and charming as ever, he greeted them warmly. "Julietta, great campaign, despite everything."

"Thanks, Peter. Great to see you, it's been a while, and congratulations on Paysimple."

"Thank you! We should talk sometime. This may surprise you but I think you're on the right track with some of the things you are saying about the economy, but there's so much room for improvement. And it's a shame to be telling those voters things that simply aren't going to happen."

She looked at him directly. "I'll keep your advice in mind, Peter. Have a great evening."

They were out the door five seconds later.

In the car Julietta was enraged. She slugged Doug's shoulder hard enough that he winced a little. "If Powell was fucking working with that fucking tool ... agggh! This is why you don't do what he did! Even if they weren't working together, this is what happens. You wind up getting associated with the worst people. Ugh."

When they finally got home they all piled into bed, and it hit

Julietta. Rolling, racking sobs emptied through her as Ayala, Doug, Ananda, and Max tried to comfort her. Not for the first time, Doug was so, so grateful for them all. Handling this together was hard enough. Handling it alone would have been awful. Julietta was too big. They all were.

9

"Babe, I can't deal." Julietta was lying on the bed staring at the ceiling, her half-packed suitcase open next to her. Doug had his feet up sideways on the couch, laptop on his lap. The sounds of Elijah and Alexander playing some complicated game involving Legos and interplanetary travel themes drifted toward them from down the hall.

"Yeah, I hear ya. It's even more of a snake pit now, isn't it? You're really sure you want to go, right? You could still cancel."

"No, I don't want to go!"

"Awww, love," he said.

"But I probably should. They asked nicely."

"Well, that's a nice change. What'd they say?"

"They want me to present the research we used in the campaign."

"Well, it's good that they were at least paying attention to you! We really broke some trail with that stuff."

"Yeah, and look how it turned out." She curled up into a ball, grabbed a pillow and starting whacking it with her fists. "Stupid Sludge Report and Powell and his stupid sleazy friends or allies or whatever he calls them. Ugh. What a mess."

"That's it though, right? Modulo the late hit and the sleaze,

88

wherever it came from, I'd be calling you Congresswoman-Elect Torres right about now. That message was connecting with people, love. I saw it. I saw it in your crowds. I saw it knocking doors. It was reaching the people we've never been able to reach. Or starting to, anyway."

"That just pisses me off even more." More fists to the pillows. He liked seeing her this fired up, at least.

"So, what's the best revenge? Go talk to a bunch of nice billionaires about what the next steps are."

"Yeah. I suppose. I'm just feeling not up for it. Imposter syndrome again, I guess. Losing is screwing with my mind."

Doug said, "You've said this enough to me, about what losing really is. I'm all for giving up on stuff that's hopeless. I've learned that lesson. This ain't that. This isn't remotely hopeless. Plus, really. It's a couple of days by the beach. There are worse fates."

"I know I know. Of course I will see about five seconds of the lovely beach. You know how it is."

"Well, maybe this time you can take it easy some. You're not pitching anything at least, just listening. That's got to be a relief, right?"

She said, "Yeah, yeah," but sounded absent, doubtful.

He said, "So. Church? Ayala is on today."

"Yeah, I'm in. Check with Max and Ananda and see how many kids you can corral up."

Doug wandered off to rally the household. The services at Fruity First were long, but no one minded. The music alternated between electronic dance, hip hop, and indie rock acts and DJs. Ayala would usually talk (she hated the word sermon) somewhere toward the middle. They'd gotten to know the founder, Von James, very well after the church's scandal-induced growth phase that let them hire Ayala.

Von had delusions of grandeur about flipping the prosperity-gospel-based megachurch script and turning Fruity First into a network of progressive megachurches. Doug and Julietta considered these delusions plenty grand and probably not all that delusional. Von grew up in Baltimore and in high school in the 80s started working on boycott, divestment & sanction campaigns against South Africa. Then he'd spent some time in India studying in an ashram, then landed in Oakland and founded a renewable energy advocacy group, which led to a brief tour in the White House. The church he and his team had built was a merging of three lineages: the black Christian church he grew up with in Baltimore, the yoga he'd studied in India and continued to study under teachers in the Bay Area, and the Bay Area integral and creative communities.

It was electronic day so the younger kids were particularly happy. Alexander was liking the live hip hop Sundays more but the littler ones just loved dancing. They bounced around on the huge rugs they'd put down to try and soften the cement floors of the cavernous warehouse. Von had picked this warehouse for the rock-bottom price mainly and for the light that filtered in from the clerestory windows in the saw-tooth roof. It was entirely devoid of creature comforts other than that, but it fit their needs perfectly.

Soon the music mellowed out into crunchy ambient. Ayala took the stage in her loosely flowing white lace shawl. Julietta glanced over at Doug watching Ayala and smiled, knowing how much he loved watching her do this. Her presence quieted the whole room, and she began.

10

Ayala's Sermon

Think, for a second here, back to a time when you felt excluded. Get kind of specific here, in your thinking: I'm not talking about feeling bad about something out in the world, like feeling bad about losing an election, even if that might be something that's present for a few of you in this moment. We'll get to that in a bit.

But to start with, I mean something more personal. Now, if you've suffered abuse, don't go back to that unless you're genuinely feeling up for it. That's definitely a form of exclusion. It's the most intense, most personal form of exclusion possible. I'm looking for something deep but not that deep here. Think about not getting invited to something, some time when you felt different and not in a good way, some time when you were an outsider to some group of people. Maybe you have to go back to middle school for the deepest hurt here —that's where it is for me!—but it could be more recent, too. Most of us experience some form of this pretty frequently if we think about it.

Now just sit here for a minute and try to remember how that felt in your body. Ordinarily when we do these things this is the part where

I tell you to breathe, right? But this time I'm not going to. Don't focus on breathing, because maybe you weren't feeling like breathing much when this happened. So, just be where you're at with it. And don't worry; I know this is unpleasant. We'll stop in a second.

OK, good. Now, flip this. Flip back to a time you felt safe, comfortable, and included. Hopefully you feel like this right now, here in our community! So, go into this moment, or think of another time where you just felt so good. Think of a time when you felt included and loved. If that's right now, great, I hope it is. But if it's some other time that's great too.

That's better, right? Now think about the experience of people in the world with these two states. For those of you who have moved ever or are immigrants, this is easier for you. Please don't think that I'm generating a false dichotomy. If you moved here from a different state, you've had a much different experience than someone who has come from another country. And if you moved voluntarily, you've had a much different experience than someone who fled because of violence or because the economy in wherever they lived collapsed, or that sort of thing.

Most of us can't imagine what refugees have gone through. Imagine losing part, or most, or all of your family in a war. Or imagine what it must feel like to have an economy fall apart around you because of laws made in a different country. There's a much larger scope to all of this. But for now what's important here is just noticing these two differences in how these states feel to you: how exclusion feels, and how inclusion feels.

The great beliefs suggest we should love the stranger

As it turns out every major religion includes treatment of the outsider as a core teaching. This is not ambiguous or subtle. It's a major theme. Really. In all of them.

In the Torah, nearly the same language is repeated in Exodus and in Leviticus. Talmudic scholars disagree on whether this idea is repeated 36 or 46 times in the Torah, but either way, it's a lot! Here's just two examples.

In Exodus 23 verse 9, it's this: "You shall not oppress a stranger, since you yourselves know the feelings of a stranger, for you also were strangers in the land of Egypt." And similarly in Leviticus, chapter 19 verse 34: "The foreigner residing among you must be treated as your native-born. Love them as yourself, for you were foreigners in Egypt. I am the LORD your God."

And in the Gospels, again it's a theme. It appears over and over, but Matthew 25, verses 34-36 is perhaps the strongest example: "Then the King will say to those on his right, 'Come, you who are blessed by my Father; take your inheritance, the kingdom prepared for you since the creation of the world. For I was hungry and you gave me something to eat, I was thirsty and you gave me something to drink, I was a stranger and you invited me in, I needed clothes and you clothed me, I was sick and you looked after me, I was in prison and you came to visit me.'" And in verse 40: "The King will reply, 'Truly I tell you, whatever you did for one of the least of these brothers and sisters of mine, you did for me."

And sure enough, this is present in the Quran too. Again it's a theme and appears in lots of places, but in chapter 4, verse 36: "Worship God and consider no one equal to Him. Be kind to your parents, relatives, orphans, the destitute, your near and distant neighbors, your companions, wayfarers, and your slaves. God does not love the proud and boastful ones."

The language behind this is fascinating. In Hebrew, the word translated as "stranger" in Exodus and Leviticus is "ger"—what Rabbi David Cooper of Kehilla Synagogue calls the "inside-outsider." That is, in his words, "someone from outside your people who is now living among you and is more vulnerable because they don't have land, or family, or deep connections in the society." Sometimes "ger" is translated as "resident alien."

And the exact same concept appears again in Arabic in the Quran as the word "ghurba." The modern poet Ghada Alatrash writes beautifully about the meaning of this here:

"The word ghurba also carries an intense feeling along with it, a melancholic feeling of longing, of nostalgia, of homesickness and separation, of a severe patriotic yearning for a place where one's heart was not only living, but also dancing to the beat of a father's or a mother's voice, to the words in grandmother's tale, to a melody from a native instrument, to the pounding of feet stamping in a group dance, to a merchant's voice shouting out the name of his merchandise in the streets of neighbourhoods, or simply, to a place where one's heart danced to the silence of a homeland's soil."

So, why don't we?

Healing this mass-scale heartbreak has been a crucial issue of building a more just, more humane society right for thousands of years. I wish I could say we've made more progress, but I think how this election cycle played out shows we have a long way to go. But since here at Fruitvale First we're all about going deeper, so let's think about why.

I'm sure if you sat here for a few minutes you could come up with a half-dozen good reasons. Or if we busted out the sharpies and poster paper notes, we could come up with 100 between us in a few minutes. We've done it in sermons before! I think the biggest two reasons are that the world seems smaller than it was, and because of changes in the economy that have made things seem a lot more insecure for a lot of people. This has led to an explosion of hard-core racism, but even this explosion has only grown their numbers a tiny bit. The vast, overwhelming majority of Americans aren't personally prejudiced against African Americans. They don't want to live in a country where our treatment of the stranger is getting worse.

And yet, we have undeniably racist outcomes, in our policies and who gets elected. This fact of racism without racists sounds a lot like this, from Grapes of Wrath, that's also quoted in Walter Wink's Engaging the Powers:

> "We're sorry. It's not us. It's the monster. The bank isn't like a man.
> Yes, but the bank is only made of men. No, you're wrong there —quite wrong there.
> The bank is something else than men. It happens that every man in a bank hates what the bank does, and yet the bank does it. The bank is something more than men, I tell you. It's the monster. Men made it, but they can't control it."

But I want to focus on one particular reason, which is about how political arguments in this country often get made. People who believe that treating strangers well have been losing a political argument by, with a few exceptions, not making one.

Consider the morality of how policies that hurt people happen. One way this is done is by conflating following the rule of law with morality. We have a long, long tradition of this in this country. An often-cited verse is from Romans, chapter 13 verse 7: "Let every person be subject to the governing authorities."

It's that simple, right? Even if the laws are militaristic and greedy, we're all subject to them, right?

What this is dismissing really the entire rest of the story of Jesus, and the major, fundamental, core and most profound teachings of Judaism and Islam as well. It's dismissing the morality of how we treat the stranger. It's dismissing the entirety of Jesus' life's story and purpose, which was dedicated to upending the deeply unjust economic system he saw. As Stephen Colbert put it, "We take the

Bible literally—even the parts that contradict the other parts."

Now, this doesn't mean we can all just ignore the law. But it does mean that, if we're going to believe and act on any parts of these three great, beautiful systems of thought, we have to fight for those laws to become kinder to the stranger. We have to fight for justice. We have to, in the words of the great warrior for civil rights, john a. powell, widen our circles of concern.

Does this mean we need open borders? Perhaps that's our goal and the direction we need to be working that direction. Imagine a world where both the motivations for migration, and the consequences of doing so, were both greatly decreased.

Like many of us here in California, I'm a migrant. I moved here from New York. This fact, and our national community's response to it—or lack of response, really!—perfectly illustrates how Dr. powell's concept of a circle of concern works.

We don't do anything to attempt to limit immigration inside the U.S.; in fact we often celebrate it, despite the cost and hassle of splitting families up geographically creates. No one accused me of depriving a more-deserving Californian of a job when I moved here! We have these attitudes because we include all Americans inside our circle of concern. Only our biases and prejudices—combined with and reinforced by some faulty economic reasoning—have so far prevented us from widening our concern and love for people in other countries trying to come here.

The world is getting smaller and forcing us to confront this. But we're not going to end domestic terrorism or achieve economic security by cutting ourselves off from the world, or by maintaining systems and laws that exploit migrants.

The beloved community, and changing laws

So, what are we going to do? Again, from Walter Wink: "A very rapid and fundamental sea change has been taking place in our worldview that has passed largely unrecognized but is everywhere felt. A new conceptual worldview is already in place, latently, and can be triggered by its mere articulation."

Mere articulation! Wink's right about the basic reality of this, but there's some danger in putting it the way he does. The "mere" there—that doesn't quite sit right with me. It makes it sounds easy, and it's not.

In a big complicated messy democracy, the new story of good news for the poor has to be told over and over, in a million conversations, in local meetings and online and via text message and knocking on people's doors, in meetings with congresspeople. Or in becoming Congress people, or even just in trying. Even though it might be unfashionable to say this, this all that organizing is: large-scale, structured storytelling. As Cesar Chavez put it, when he was asked how to organize, "First you talk to one person, and then another, and then another." Or as another teacher put it, "Follow Me, and I will make you become fishers of people."

Laws matter. Profoundly. Overwork, traffic, mass incarceration, gun violence, wealth inequality, poverty—all these things wedge us in the first step of fear, separation, and illusion. It's a great cycle: The more the laws yoke us to the system, the harder it is to change them. Laws can be changed, but we're stuck in this cycle:

Fear creates illusion of a sense of separation.
The illusion of separation creates a sense of fragility.
Fragility creates othering and domination.
Domination and othering creates injustice.
Injustice creates more fear!

Unjust laws and unwise budget choices made by our democracy are byproducts of this cycle of toxicity and injustice and fear. But the laws are just a byproduct, so how do we break up this cycle? Wink again: "Any attempt to transform a social system without addressing both its spirituality and its outer forms is doomed to failure." How do we address these inner forms?

The answer in short, is the work of doing love, the work of building inclusive community. It's building spaces where that feeling in the place we went to at the beginning of my talk today is undeniable, where that warmth of feeling included is available.

Audre Lorde gets at the same idea: "Caring for myself is not self-indulgence, it is self-preservation and that is an act of political warfare."

Self-care itself IS the work. And doing the work—when it's going well—can charge you up as well as anything.

As the writer and spiritual teacher Kristie Dahlia Home has written, "This is what we mean when we speak of spiritual alchemy: emotion arises. We could become lost in the story of that emotion. But if we go back to the root, which is always love, we can shine right out past fear into more love, into cherishing, into the glorious beauty of the shining, endless NOW. Impermanence is terrifying; the mind cannot grasp it. Impermanence is also that which makes the eternal now so beautiful, so beautiful."

That reality is the basis of our answer to the fragility part of the cycle. The process of decolonization has to start between your ears, and in your heart. The integral, resilient worldview says to us: Be present, and your heart will tell you it's not all about you; and that separation between you and the other? It's nothing more than an illusion. And the reality of inclusion feels a lot better than the separation.

From First John, chapter 4 verse 18: "There is no fear in love. But perfect love drives out fear, because fear has to do with punishment. The one who fears is not made perfect in love."

The choice before us

I can't quite say there's a silver lining to a loss. There's too much on the line, and to describe it as such negates the experience many people are likely to have over the next few years because of this. People have said, Well, we'll survive this, because we always have before.

But the fact is that many people haven't survived. People will die in wars that will be started or not stopped, or from pollution, or from the increases in climate-related social upheaval, or from terrorists emboldened by extremists in government. As our laws and choices are shaped by a narrowing circle of concern—it's only the wealthy that matter, or anyone with a job—it's not just the most vulnerable whose lives are at stake with these issues, it's our own lives too.

That being said, losses do offer lessons and clarity that can't easily be learned any other way. The paths before us have been thrown into sharper relief. We can stay with the beliefs we have now, or we can embark on a new direction.

We can choose to leave ever-increasing amounts of wealth in private hands, or we can awaken to the reality that wealth is created by systems more than by individuals and that a democracy with good news for the poor as its core defining purpose is going to spend wealth with more justice than a kleptocracy will.

We can choose to end the poisoning of the climate and protect our world for our children, or we can pass the problems on to them for a few more years of jobs and profits.

We can choose to do the hard, but fascinating and deeply rewarding, work of how to live in truly diverse communities, or we can dismiss that work as nothing more than political correctness and live lives less rich because of that decision.

From Luke 14, verse 13: "But when you give a banquet, invite the poor, the crippled, the lame, the blind, and you will be blessed."

Thich Nhat Hanh, when asked what the "best" mantra is—after acknowledging the slight absurdity of the question—said that it is

"Darling, I am here for you."
It's time for us to be here for the world.
Go, fight hard, and love each other.

11

A fter her talk, Ayala sat back down. Doug grinned at her and she looked up at him, with her usual look that said "That was ok, right?" He laughed, nodding encouragingly.

After the service, the five grownups schlepped the four kids into two cars and walked out two hours later, blinking in the sunshine. Ayala's sermon had been about the wisdom of shifting tactics when the moment called for it. Julietta said, dryly, "Well, what a weird coincidence. How could she possibly have known?"

Doug giggled. "Beats me!" She elbowed him, and he said, "It must be a sign from above."

Max said, "I don't know how, but even as a confirmed agnostic I feel good after those services."

Doug said, "It's Ayala! She really is a magician."

Julietta made a funny awkward cough. Doug turned to her: "So what do you think? You're going, right?"

"Yeah, I give up."

He said, "Mmmm: surrender. I like it."

THE DISTRICT 12 Alliance was a group of large donors that had splintered off from a different, larger organization of progressive donors some years earlier. The D12A was exclusively and deliberately tackling economic issues: poverty to inequality to sustainability to the struggling, evaporating middle class. The larger, previous organization had largely failed to fund economics work. There were many reasons why this was, but it basically came down to a significant subset of donors not seeing economic reform as a priority over other more easily understood feel-good causes like voting rights, the environment, and LGBTQ struggles.

The strategy the D12 took was to go wide more than deep and fund as much of the economic reform ecosystem as they could. They were supporting groups doing everything from deep academic research to on the ground organizing: Wonderful groups like Demos, the Roosevelt Institute, People's Action and the Institute for New Economic Thinking were just a few of them. The D12 liked funding groups already supported by organized labor, which helped keep the groups accountable to communities.

Out of the myriad ways organizers described building power, the analysis Julietta liked most was one of the simplest: Monviolent political power in a democracy has three sources and three dimensions. People. Story. Money. That's it. And the dimensions were equally clear: dimension 1 is stopping bad stuff, dimension 2 is starting and winning your own objectives, and dimension 3 is changing underlying worldviews, changing the underlying terrain that political battles were pitched on. Given the jaw-dropping scale of the money being spent opposing their agenda, groups like the D12 were absolutely essential for progress across all three dimensions.

But it was still a constant an uphill fight. Part of it was straight-up lack of resources: The millions they were spending were still dwarfed by the budgets of the big DC conservative think tanks and an armada of smaller state organizations. Even years of abject, unmistakable policy failures hadn't slowed the momentum of organizations like the American Enterprise Institute, the Heritage Institute, and the Club for Growth. On a good day, the D12-aligned groups could still notch wins, or at least fight the conservative groups to a draw. They had a force multiplier they were able to leverage to make their limited resources go farther: Their policies worked for everyone, not just for the rich, and they had the data and research to prove it.

But there were two gaps in the progressive economic ecosystem that persisted: One was around ideas marketing, and the other was around accountability. Ideas marketing was the cornerstone of dimension 3 power: a layer of research into how people understand concepts and change their worldviews over the long term. There was some degree of consensus in the D12 (which Julietta shared) that ideas marketing was manipulative, too much like regular marketing, and maybe above all, an expensive money pit with uncertain results.

The accountability that was needed was something like what Club for Growth or the NRA had managed to accomplish over years: These groups had established a clearly defined set of issues and would gleefully and aggressively find and fund primary opponents for representatives that didn't deliver votes on those issues. This was also viewed as an expensive, risky bet; elections are complicated, subject to lots of variables, and almost always expensive. Since the D12 had less clarity on issues, it was often less clear in primaries whom they should support, so the mixed messages and tepid support Julietta received from a few individuals in her campaign was common. Rafael hadn't said this in her invitation, but she suspected her presence there was part of his plan to illustrate what the ramifications of this lack of clarity were.

In Julietta's view, the D12 folks were some of the best Americans alive. Not many of the wealthy had the courage to face the core paradoxes of reforming the system that had been so personally beneficial to them. These folks had. There were a hundred and fifty of them; mostly new money but some old. About half had made their money in startups and technology, belying the common misperception that new tech wealth was generating only libertarian acolytes for Peter Dixon. These days, there were more socialists working at Google than libertarians.

Their yearly conference was three intense days of pitches, research presentations, and deal-making. Even though she liked and respected the people and found the actual process exciting, it was also frustrating and exhausting and very much at her edge. She'd been just outside the D12 orbit with her own work with the Women's Strategy Network, which occasionally collaborated with D12.

But there was a good reason their collaborations were only occasional. While at the insistence of one of the Black founders of the organization, they'd baked aggressive steps to face down internal institutional racism, sexism, and classism into the founding charter, and they'd done a lot of genuine hard work on this as an organization. But Julietta and every other woman she knew who had grappled with the D12 still considered it a bit of a boys club.

As the plane landed at Miami International, Julietta felt her body already starting to tighten defensively.

"Men." She thought.

She rolled over in bed the next morning, mildly hung over from the opening night schmoozing in the bar, and texted Doug. "Oh love, why why why why why why" before realizing it was 5:00 am back in Oakland. She thought briefly there was a bare chance he was up. She rolled onto her back and stared at the ceiling for a few minutes, until the awful dawning sense that she was definitely awake and no way going back to sleep fully set in.

She groaned and got up, briefly considering the only two options she knew that would provide any measure of hangover relief. The hard path was some kind of exercise. The easy one was a huge, bacon-oriented breakfast. But her stomach shuddered a little at the thought of the breakfast so she walked out on the balcony. One look at the long, white beach was all she needed.

She gulped down some water and decided it was a day to ignore her ambivalent confidence in her body. She changed into running shorts and a running bra, guessed she didn't need shoes and soon was in front of the hotel feeling cool sand between her toes. The closed beachfront bar sat empty facing the sand, with rows of chairs and folded umbrellas stretching out toward the white line of frothy surf backed by the gulf stream purple of the early dawn Atlantic ocean. She dropped into a couple warm-up yoga poses that her stomach seemed to copy move for move, although it slowly settled as she started moving.

She slowed down into the yoga, and her mind flitted through its usual patterns: a sharp pang of missing the kids, Elijah and Nora first, but then the rest of the pack of them, and then a tingling wave of pure, crystalline excitement and hope that you can only get from thinking about babies when she thought about Ayala and Doug's. Ayala's pregnancy had amplified their collective feelings of compassion beyond anything she'd imagined. Just a flood of happy, fuzzy feelings every time she thought about both of them. They'd expected things to get crunchy but figured they'd been through enough at that point to handle it, but instead, even through the genuine insanity of her campaign it had smoothed the connections out between all of them. She rode a wave of intense gratitude through it and smiled to herself, dropping into her favorite hip-opening pose.

Work stuff came up next. She thought through the presentation she was delivering that afternoon but decided her stress level for this one was pretty close to zero. She ordinarily would have been intimidated by the collective mental firepower of the folks she was going in front of, but something had shifted. It just didn't feel like as much of an edge. Only a few of the D12 had run for office, but she'd been part of the conversations about the amount of respect they had for those who did. When it came down to it, the one thing this community shared was a bedrock, bone-deep love of and respect for democracy. Maybe, she thought, some of them wouldn't get it, but this was the shift: She just cared less. She was going to make the case for the connection between their hopes and the work she'd done. For her it was a straight, bright line of purpose. Having a chance to do this work she felt so called to was the essence of true freedom. She focused on that bright line, relaxed deeper into the pose, and her mind went blissfully quiet. She did a few more leg stretches, unfolding out with her mind clear, and then started to run up the beach.

This part of the beach was deserted but for a few other distant figures. The mental clutter came back pretty quickly, and she thought about how much she had disliked running and still had mixed feelings about it, but then she thought about how ridiculous that was given the setting, and—the kids came to mind again—the preciousness of time to herself. She set the timer on what Doug called her nerdy watch (another of his quirky turn-ons) and settled into a slow pace, the rhythmic waves crashing to her right as she took off to the north.

A few minutes up the beach, someone was running toward her. As he got closer she gasped a bit: It was Rafael Somos himself. She smiled at him and hesitated but didn't stop; he had headphones in and was barefoot too but didn't seem like he was slowing down. He seemed a bit surprised or confused but smiled back, either at her or in mutual enjoyment of the gorgeous place to run, or maybe both.

She knew he'd been a hesitant participant in D12, or at least there was a perception that his level of involvement was less than he would have been capable of given the size of the family fortune he was sitting on. But there was always loose talk and sniping in the group around this from those who knew what their internal family process was. As a wealthy donor and friend once explained to her, the reason things were complicated with family money was simple: They were families. She'd said, imagine your family, but with all that money, and how that would go.

And, Julietta thought, no one quite knew if the D12 was even a worthwhile investment yet. There wasn't even much agreement on how to measure their impact to determine if it was. And her loss hadn't exactly helped their case, at least so far. She was just hopeful some learning would come of it, at least.

She pushed herself a little farther, not turning around until she'd been running for twnty minutes. She wanted to talk to Felicia but couldn't remember if she was flying in today or later; Felicia had been a proponent of the original schism that formed the D12 and had consulted on the initial strategy but had been less involved lately, partially of her own accord and partially after a series of ridiculous microaggressions at one of the previous meetings. Julietta made a mental note to text her when she got back, then tried to dump all the work stuff out of her mind and just run for the last bit, enjoying the waves and the deepening pink of the sky as the sun rose over the ocean.

She got back and txted Felicia and sent one to Doug too, "whoa i ran into rafael somos running on the beach. didn't talk though"

Doug wrote back shortly "you went running on the beach? pics? :P" She snapped a pic of herself and sent it to him with the caption, "i'm all hot and sweaty now."

He wrote, "for rafael or for me? this is grant somos's kid, right? supermegacrazywealthy? is he cute?"

Julietta thought for a second. She wasn't sure. "some? maybe? i don't know. i think i might like his brain, you know how that is for me."

Doug thought, uh-oh, but smiled too and sent back, "ay yi yi. think it's a thing?"

She couldn't tell if he was actually concerned. She knew that, fundamentally, their relationship was constructed on a solid foundation of security and compersion, the hidden-from-view word describing the opposite of jealousy, that feeling of spreading happiness from something good happening to someone you love. It was the byproduct of years of work and their mutual love for Ayala and the rest of their extended network. But even after all those years and all that work, he'd admitted on occasion that her traveling was still a little hard for him. So she said, "awww love. i have no idea, but you know you have nothing to worry about right."

Doug wrote back, "i know i know. just missing you. time to schlep the kiddos. knock 'em dead this afternoon."

Felicia txted back that she was around, Julietta asked if she was up for a last minute strategy session to go over her talk and they agreed to meet.

The morning sessions were mostly panels, dissections of election results and updates on longer-term campaigns. Julietta tried to pay attention but the loss was weighing on her heavily, which always brought up the shame and fear from the Sludge Report-led attacks on her family, and that in turn sometimes brought her back in touch with the multiplied suffering insight she'd had that otherwise-glorious afternoon with Ayala. The cognitive dissonance—that gap again—of sitting in a room full of billionaires and being in touch with the multiplied suffering of the people she'd worked so hard to represent at the same time made her feel a little dizzy.

Rafael was sitting across the room, but they made eye contact and smiled at each other, then kept doing the whole occasionally making eye contact in an ambiguous and possibly slightly flirtatious way. "Yeah, Doug," she thought to herself, "he's kind of cute." It was unfamiliar and she realized another thing that had shifted; this was the first D12 conference she'd been to since her campaign, which meant this was the first one she'd been to where she and Doug were out as having an open relationship.

At lunch she approached him, "I think I could do with a run like that every morning."

"Me too! Glorious, wasn't it? It's so good to see you." He put his hand out and she shook it, their eyes connecting, and he held onto it, "Thank you so much for your other run, too. Your campaign, I mean. I'm excited about hearing the details this afternoon."

She smiled, wondering how much of the awkwardness was just him, and how much was attraction. "Thanks! I'm really grateful for your support Rafael. I'm sorry it didn't work out."

"Well, you gave it a hell of a shot, and that's what I was hoping for. I'm not quite sure what some of the other Alliance members were looking for. We didn't invest in a lot of races this cycle, even the modest investment the few of us made in your race was unusual. So, I suggested to the conference committee that you should come talk because I think you took the most risks in your message."

Julietta gulped nervously at this, "It sounds like the appreciation of those risks isn't all that evenly shared."

He said, "No, it's not." She wanted to know more but this didn't seem like the time or the place for it.

"Well, at any rate, thanks for getting me in here. I'm really feeling the loss today, but hoping that telling the story is going to help."

"I was wondering how you've been. My family and I are no strangers to these kinds of attacks, unfortunately." The Somos family was a long-time target of threats of all kinds, particularly anti-Semitism. "Although the level of vitriol and personal attack on your family was unfamiliar even to us. Sexism seems to add another layer of nastiness."

She realized she hadn't talked to anyone beyond her close circle who had been through something similar, and it felt good. "I'm glad that part is over. It was awful. I'm still trying to make sense of it."

He said, "I've never been able to. I meditate pretty regularly, a little mindfulness and compassion practice that helps me out a lot. It's not difficult for me to hold our intelligent opponents inside the circle of compassion I try to extend to all beings. Someone like Peter Dixon. Sure, I understand where he is coming from, even if he seems pompous sometimes or like his worldview is all built around either fear or a story about how he got to where he got that is more about making him feel comfortable. Or even more easily, the people in this group I disagree with, who at least I feel like we share a goal with. But the serious hatred? The people who offer death threats? I have a much harder time with them."

Julietta couldn't hide how impressed she was. She said, "On some level me too. Although, in a lot of cases the anger is justified. They've just been lied to, so they get mad at the wrong things. And our side hasn't exactly been great at telling a story about what folks SHOULD be angry at, about why things are the way they are. Which we tried to do in the campaign. At least a little."

Rafael nodded, "A valuable experiment, at least. And if you can extend even a little compassion to the truly vitriolic, you're a better person than I am. Anyway. Good luck this afternoon."

As her session was about to start she texted Doug from the audience. "ok rafael is cute. had an ok conversation with him. about to go on. really fucking nervous. this is worse than pitching something because the dough is already spent! :("

He wrote back with a bunch of emoji hearts. She figured he was in the middle of something, leaned over to Felicia and whispered, "I may need to throw up."

Felicia said, "Breathe, lady. Don't worry, these guys are pussycats. They're just glad you're willing to come here and talk."

Julietta replied, "I sure hope you're right."

The room was full. It seemed more full than it had been in the morning, but she wasn't sure if that was true. She had her preferred speaking setup, at least: no podium, a tiny wireless mic instead of a big handheld one, and a tiny remote clicker for her slides. She started her presentation out like this: "I am sorry to be here to report another footnote in the great American habit of letting racism and sexism shred progress on building an equitable economy." It went well from there, she thought. She laid out the substance of their policy: strong public investment, and how they could pay for it, then got into how they approached the message development process and why the fire in the message was a critical component. She hoped laying that part out in some detail would inoculate her against too many questions. And she briefly summarized the family structure research, and the Sludge Report attacks and how they thought that had affected the media dynamics around the campaign.

The first question was from someone she didn't know well, an older woman whom Julietta had once tried to recruit for the Women's Strategy Network but had never gotten far with. Real-estate money, she thought she remembered. "Since we're here in private and I have a feeling a lot of people don't know how this works, could you give us a few minutes of explanation of your family? This ... polyamory thing?"

Not what Julietta was expecting, but understandable. And if this was how they wanted to use her time, she was happy to talk about this rather than economics. "Well, some of this came out in the campaign, thanks to Sludge, but I'll recap: Doug and I are married but have an open relationship. We identify ourselves as nonmonogamous or having an open relationship more than polyamorous, but the distinctions aren't super important. We have our two kids: Elijah is seven and Nora is turning two in a few months, and we're both involved with a woman, Ayala, who has a four-year-old named Avi and is five months pregnant now with her and Doug's baby. And I've been romantically involved with Max for years. He is married to Ananda, and they have a nine-year-old, Alexander. So we have five grownups in the house, and will have five kids in a few weeks.

"There's another important part of this setup, which is that financially our house is modeled after an Israeli kibbutz: It's basically

111

a small cooperative enterprise where the money that comes in is shared equally amongst all of us, and we do our best to tear down distinctions between emotional and paid labor. So, part of how I was able to run was that my husband has been working part-time for pay and sharing child-care duties with the rest of the house."

The same woman said, "Wow. I don't know if that's the best thing I've ever heard of or the worst."

Both the crowd and Julietta laughed, and she said, "We get that response a lot. It works for us, incredibly well. I don't think I could have run without knowing that the kids were surrounded by so many loving adults while I was out at events and knocking on doors nearly every night. We tried to involve the kids in the campaign as much as we could, but of course Nora is not even two. We think the older kids got a lot out of the experience, but all of them are certainly glad to have me around again more. You're probably familiar with bell hooks' work on communities and revolutionary parenting: We're hardly the first people to give this a shot, women of color have been doing it for centuries. But we're definitely a bit unusual for our demographics."

Her questioner nodded, but then seemed to remember something and said, "So, what made you think you'd be able to keep all of this private through the campaign?"

Julietta bristled inside but kept cool. "We didn't. In our early go-versus-no-go research we started to see the pattern that if it came out it wouldn't hurt us. I still think that was true. The line of attack that worked on us wasn't about my family."

The woman said, "It seems obviously not true to me. Particularly since you waited so long and let the story get ahead of you."

Julietta hesitated, "We have research to back it up that I'd be willing to share with the group. It is …" Julietta gulped down a quick breath, and went slowly through this part, choosing her words carefully, "It is possible how it came out and how we responded wasn't optimal, yes. But we thought we faced a real risk of blowing it up worse. And to be honest, we either misjudged the character of my opponent, or we misjudged the sophisticated and aggressive unscrupulousness of the forces that were supporting him." She thought back to the D12 raising attacks on her message right at that moment and how that threw them off their game and felt a bit queasy. She wasn't sure if her urge to not admit the mistake to this person was a legitimate strategic choice or if she was just pissed off and digging in.

The woman addressed the crowd now, "It seems like there's a lesson here about the kind of research we need to do on candidates before we start supporting them."

The questioner probably didn't mean to trigger Julietta off all the shit her family had been through, but at this point Julietta had had enough. She was pissed. She wanted to fire back and call out what felt like slut-shaming to her, but she took a breath and simply said, "That sounds like you are recommending making decisions about who can and can't run based on how their families look."

She said, "I just want this group to be deliberate about making good investments, is all."

Rafael stepped up at this point, "Maybe we can take this discussion offline. Julietta, could we talk about the economic vision and plan your team came up with?"

She was actually relieved to get into the economics at this point. She could feel the adrenaline still bouncing around her system but set it aside and did the best she could.

Afterwards, Rafael found her in the hall as she was headed back to her room. She said to him, "Well, that was awful. But I suppose could have been worse. What do you think?"

He said, "It is what it is. It could have been worse!" She laughed a little but looked away, feeling irritated she'd bothered coming. He said, "Julietta I have a request. One of my dad's yachts is docked in a harbor not far from here. I've invited a few of the more progressive and more friendly donors up to it for a quiet dinner. Would you be interested in coming with? It will be mellow, not like that session. Six or seven of us. People I trust."

She felt done with everything, not like going to dinner at all. And yet, she was pretty sure there was no way she was going to say no. She had a brief moment of curiosity about what Doug and Max were going to think of this development, then came back to the moment and said, "Sounds great. When and where?"

"End of the C dock of the South Miami marina. My boat is the Renegade. Look for the tallest mast, you won't miss it. Anytime after 7."

The tallest mast? Now she really wondered what Doug was going to think.

―――――――――――

12

As she stepped aboard, Julietta silently thanked Doug for the couple of times over the years he'd dragged her out sailing. She may not have been able to back the *Renegade* out of the slip by herself and head her out across the Gulf Stream to the Bahamas, but at least she knew starboard from port. She had more mixed feelings about the fact that Doug would be completely losing his mind at the size and loveliness of this particular boat. As she approached the dock she saw the silhouette of a figure that looked familiar but she couldn't quite place, pacing slowly in the dark far toward the bow, engrossed on a call. She guessed the boat was at least eighty feet long.

As she entered the main cabin, Rafael said, "Welcome aboard. Thanks for joining us, Julietta."

She recognized a few of them and at first glance thought all or nearly all of them had been supporters. And she realized, not all were billionaires. Some were staff and activists and organizers she knew from other contexts. Rafael continued, "We know the overall reception to what you've been up to has been mixed; but, Julietta, thank you for not just running but for the way you ran. We realize how difficult that must have been both for you and for your family, and you can count everyone as deeply grateful. Thank you. Ah wait— before we toast, where'd Erykah go?"

Someone said she was making a call, and Rafael leaned out of the door in the bulkhead, beckoning to her. A few seconds laster Erykah appeared behind him, mischievously smiling at Julietta.

Rafael picked up where he'd left off. "To Julietta!"

Stepping onto a yacht into a roomful of applauding billionaires, top organizers, and a person whose first impression had been to insult her was not how she expected the rest of today to go after this afternoon's session. Rafael put a glass of champagne in her hand.

After the applause had settled Rafael said, "Julietta, please relax and enjoy yourself. I'll be cooking this evening. Just have a few things to throw on the grill."

She grinned at him, and then at the crowd, and started chatting her way through the spacious cabin as he disappeared back toward the open galley adjacent to the cabin. She was struck that Rafael seemed to have managed to pull together the mellow and down-to-earth caucus of the D12. Everyone was friendly and genuine, and she could feel herself starting to almost relax, except for Erykah's presence, hanging there in the back of her mind like a word she couldn't remember.

After mingling a bit but managing to avoid Erykah, she slipped out of the cabin and found her way out to the back deck where a large grill hung out over the water. Rafael wasn't kidding about cooking: He was flipping a bunch of veggies over with tongs as she approached.

"Hi, sailor, what's for dinner?"

"Oh hi, Julietta, you found me. Bunch of veggies and filet mignon. I did cheat a little, the crew chief cooks too, and he threw together some sauces before he left."

She said, "I'm impressed you cook."

116

"I find it really helps me think. I feel weird it I don't do it."

Julietta said, "I think you're in a minority here."

"About the cooking, or the thinking? Or the being weird, for that matter?"

She laughed, "Maybe all three!"

He flipped a few of the veggies into a serving tray and pulled the steaks off onto another one. "Help me carry?"

Julietta said, "Of course, but I have a question about one of your guests. You know Erykah. Do you know offhand if she worked with Powell's campaign?"

Rafael stopped and looked at her. "Not that I know of. All I know is a bit about some of her research on marketing, persuasion and neurophysiology, which was intriguing stuff, and why I included her. Why? You know her?"

"Not really. But we met and chatted briefly at Powell's victory party. She had some rather pointed feedback for me on my campaign."

Rafael said, "I've noticed she can come off a little intense. Crap. I seem to have created a muddle."

She laughed at this, wondering if he meant to reference *A Room With a View*, one of her favorite movies. "OK, well I will can handle it. I won't start out assuming the witness is hostile at least."

He looked at her. "You seem rather capable of handling things."

She said, "I am, it's just been a bit much lately is all. Let's go eat."

She grabbed two of the trays and they headed in to the long table in the center of the cabin. Julietta put hers down and strode over to Erykah and said, "Hello, good to see you again." Erykah said, "You too!" and seemed genuine, but Rafael mercifully interrupted with a "Let's eat, everyone."

The seating was a bit tight but more pleasingly intimate than uncomfortable. The dinner conversation started out light. Talking about the conference, of course, and the various characters. A little

117

gossipy but in the respectful and appreciative, even loving, way she'd noticed a lot of longtime political operators took on.

After the meal, Rafael disappeared back into the galley and then reappeared with bottle of scotch and glasses. "Everyone, I did invite you here tonight for a reason. The one thing you all have in common is that I know you are all share a transformational vision for the potential of this country. You've all taken very different paths to get to that vision, which is why I'm so delighted to be bringing you together."

"So, my question is: what's next? And Julietta, I hate to put you on the spot, but I feel like you possibly have more of a concrete idea for this than anyone."

She was momentarily surprised at his kindness. This whole night seemed like it was designed to throw her off balance. But she came back to feeling at home with most this crew and got her footing, "I wish I did, Rafael. I've taken this loss hard, and I think it's still too early for me to even think about anything concrete. But if you think it'd be helpful, I could go into some of the strategic background that went into our campaign."

Rafael said, "Please!"

"The basic analysis was around systems renewal. We preferred to say *renewal* rather than *failure* since in a lot of cases the systems aren't failing, they're limping along or even mostly functional. Or in some cases, the system is functioning exactly as has been intended—how we're basically a police state, or think of the prison industrial complex, or student debt—but it's built on deep injustices and making people less free. In some cases, systems are failing and there are needs for urgent, even emergency, changes: Policing and gun safety are good examples of this, as are climate and energy. But in a lot of cases they're just not optimized. So, we looked at everything from food systems to education to immigration to trade rules, taxes, prisons, workplace structures to transportation and energy to what have you.

Let alone the backdrop of the military industrial complex." She felt like she was rambling but looked around at the crowd, and she hadn't lost anyone.

"So, we decided, running for Congress was a shitty way to approach any of these problems. But maybe at this point it was the least shitty. And possibly at least worth trying. The big challenge is how to get the media and the electorate focused on the opportunities around these transformations rather than on distractions."

Rafael said, "Like cute pictures of candidates at sexy parties."

Julietta laughed. "For one example, sure. We approached the campaign as a learning exercise, so win or lose we'd get at least something helpful out of it. Which we certainly did. My wonderful staff and I are pulling together a report on what we learned, we're just waiting for final election results to pull it all together." Julietta stopped short of offering to share the report, in part because Erykah seemed to be on the edge of saying something. Erykah was holding back for some reason, but Julietta could sense it and wasn't helping calm the edginess she felt just from her presence there.

Rafael said, "Thanks for that summary. I'm definitely curious to see the deeper reporting as you get it." Nods all around as people nursed their scotches. Rafael continued, "This brings us to the question at hand. What next?"

It was quiet. The boat rocked gently. The rigging hummed slightly as a light breeze spun over the marina.

Julietta thought back to the beginning of the campaign. Back beyond it, the endless conversations she and Doug were always having about crazy ideas. Sometimes they'd get stoned and just bullshit each other endlessly. The heart of their romance was their shared commitment to the great project of Tikkun Olam, of improving and supporting each other and improving the world. Banter like that was one of their favorite ways to have fun.

She decided, what the hell, and said, "There was something Doug

119

and I came up with at one point that might be relevant. Sort of a ... pilot project. A way to try out big, systemic change. But in a pretty isolated, even reversible way. Although our guess is it would never be rolled back once it was started. And we're not talking about some kind of tiny or isolated utopia; most of what we're proposing isn't even that different from how the current system works. It's more about distribution: that old William Gibson line, *the future is already here, it's just not evenly distributed yet.* All the systems changes would be based on the current systems; just take the current infrastructure, find the places where innovation is already happening, and spread those changes faster."

"Ohhhh. Yeah." Rafael's eyebrows went up. He said, "Can you give us an example?"

Julietta thought back to the vision she'd had in the wood with Ayala and wondered how she was ever going to describe that to this crowd. She thought for a second, "OK, take education. Schools in California run the gamut from high-performing to underperforming, but we looked into this and were surprised at what we found. A lot of them are pretty great, even outperforming the tough socioeconomic hands that a lot of them have been dealt. So, let's look at what's working where it is working, and talk about where we want things to go, and then design policies around that. In some cases they need money, and revenue has to be part of it, but in lots of cases the money is already there. You can go down the list: Healthcare works in some places, doesn't in others. It's the same for energy systems, for transportation, for work cultures, for urban planning. The solutions are all out there, we just haven't been focused on implementing them."

Rafael said, "So, practically, how would this work?"

"Well, you need to find some kind of territory to run it in. Maybe a small state. It doesn't have to be somewhere in the U.S. We always wanted to do California; it'd be a good fit in terms of the demographics and psychology and historical narrative of the state. And in a way, Trump and Trumpism have made this more of an opportunity, not less. The only problem is, the campaign would be ludicrously expensive there."

Rafael said, "What if money was no object?" Julietta wasn't sure if he meant it or if it was a thought experiment. She got a little chill up her spine, imagining what the ramifications of that might be.

She simply said, "In that case, California might be a great place to try it out. We've been calling it Democratic Capitalism. It's definitely not capitalism, but it's not really socialism, either, so that's what we settled on calling it. I'm sure Erykah could come up with something better."

Erykah took that as her opening. She said, "Well, first of all, I love the substance of this idea." Julietta felt 100% certain that this was the beginning of a shit sandwich. "But with the set of neurolinguistic underpinnings of the California electorate's current worldview, it's not going to happen."

Julietta was briefly irritated that she left off the second, positive part of the traditional shit sandwich construction. She said, "You think the voters are happy with the rate that unemployment is increasing? Or climate, or energy, or traffic, or a dozen other systems? We have data that suggests otherwise."

Erykah said, "I'm saying nothing of the sort. But I am saying that if your data was so good, we'd be calling you Congresswoman-elect."

Julietta glared at her. "Well, if your preferred candidate hadn't abandoned his principles on the last weekend, we probably would be."

Erykah laughed. "You think Powell was my preferred candidate? Ha!" Julietta looked at her, not knowing where this was going. "I was just at his party because a girlfriend of mine wanted company. And I'm generally pretty happy to drink the booze of the guy I didn't vote for. Or in this case, to have a drink with the person who I did vote for."

Julietta wasn't sure what to do with the compliment, and luckily Rafael was ready to bail her out and change course, "Erykah, what would a campaign like that look like?"

Erykah paused. Now she was surprised and put on her back foot. "Well, I'd have to give that some thought. But I can definitely think of a few directions I'd go. Some media tactics I'd want to try."

Rafael said, "Advertising of some kind?"

Erykah said, "No, no. Probably not. Or not a big part it. More like a combination of deep qualitative research and content testing pushed out through the machine learning back-end my firm has been building. I could pull some ideas together."

Rafael smiled, "I'd like that. I'm definitely curious to hear more." He smiled at Erkyah and she thought she detected a bit of the same awkwardness he'd had with her, and it hit her that he was probably a little turned on by both of them. "Funny how things change. I just got into this work because of my concern about climate, but it's increasingly clear to me how all the issues are tied together, and what it's going to take to move things forward."

They conversation shifted more into stories of other campaigns, and Julietta was grateful to be out of the spotlight. Rafael moved to wrap things up eventually. The kibbitzing continued and at one point, Rafael whispered to her and asked her if she'd be up for staying. She nodded discreetly, then moved off toward another knot of people to chat with.

To her surprise Erykah was one of the first to leave, and no one seemed to notice that Julietta wasn't. Julietta's attraction to Rafael was growing but fully in check; she had no idea what his situation was, and she didn't want to take the chance of fouling up what was looking like an interesting collaboration.

As soon as everyone was out he went back into one of the lockers and pulled out another bottle and put it on the table. "We're not chartered under the British Flag but we try to keep things civilized anyway. Care for a rum ration?"

Julietta hesitated since she'd already had a little scotch and still had a buzz from the Erykah situation. "Rafael, this has been fun. But I have to stop talking work for a little bit. I'm still recovering from the campaign. This has all been rather a lot faster coming at me than I was really quite ready for. I'm glad you're excited about the pilot project, but I hope you know I'm probably not up for leading it. It's been quite a year for us."

He said, "I completely understand," although she felt a bit like he said it in a way that was just letting her not have to make a decision immediately. He shifted gears. "Well, Julietta I agree. Enough work. Tell me about yourself. I'm awfully curious about your relationship. I hope that's an OK topic."

"Of course. And I'm the first to admit, there's lots to be curious about. But I'm curious about you. You're young and busy but I imagine get a lot of interest? You involved with anyone?"

He said, "Not at the moment. Good guess on the busy factor. But this is partially why I'm asking. It seems like trying your way might solve a problem I'm having. Or a couple of problems, even. I meet a lot of people, you know? You'd think it would be easy and I'm certainly not lacking in options, but nothing is working for me right now. In part because I've always felt like there was something more out there."

She said, "I bet you have options!" She was openly flirting at this point. He seemed not to know how to handle it, and she was charmed by this, so she said, "I could talk about this all night and we can sometime if you want, but not when we're at a work thing. And I have to admit, I kind of want to see your boat. Care to give me a tour?"

"Sure." He stood up and took her hand. OK, he's got a little smooth in there underneath the layers of awkward. Good. It had been a while since she'd charmed a younger man but she thought she'd need a little spark to work with.

They wandered forward through the cabins. It seemed immense, but the only thing she could compare it to was the little cabin cruisers she and Doug had chartered a couple of times. It had that understated, perfectly designed feeling that read to her as evidence of serious money, much more than gleaming bars, gold fixtures, and flat screen TVs in every corner.

They were in a tight passageway heading back under the cockpit toward the aft cabin, and she stopped him as soon as they emerged. This was the nicest cabin she'd seen. Most of it was taken over by a very large, very comfortable looking bed. She stood close to him and looked up at him, "So, there's one thing you should know about Doug and me. Or make it two. First, if something happens between you and me, that's OK." She felt him tense up, breathing in quickly. "But second, we do like going slow, too."

He smiled. "Mmmm. I like slow, too." They kissed, lightly at first, but it got lightning hot fast. She liked how he kissed. It was hungry and a little sloppy but felt good and he seemed to have not much in the way of feeling his desire. He was strong, too: he pressed her up against the side of the cabin, then grabbed her under her ass and moved her up onto a shelf. She wrapped her legs around him and shot desire back at him, grabbing his ass and pulling his hips toward her, grinding herself up against him. She felt him get instantly hard against her, and she slowed things down. She leaned back, dropped her head back as he started kissing her neck and was moving his hands underneath her loose blouse.

She said, "Mmmm, so good. I want to know Rafael, how long have you wanted me."

Not stopping kissing her neck he said, "I had no idea this was a possibility. Even knowing you were open. So I never let myself go past my first impression."

124

"What was what?"

"I saw you speak a couple of years ago, at a conference. You were talking about Reflective Democracy, really pitching it hard. And well. But you were frustrated. Seeing how much you wanted it was hot."

She dug her hands into him again, grinding her crotch up and down on him as he moaned. More long, slow kisses as time slowed to a crawl. After a long lovely moment of this she pulled back and whispered into his ear, "I fucking hate injustice." He twitched under her, writhing and kissing her some more. After a long, breathless kiss she pulled back and whispered again, "Don't kill me. This is fun and I hate to leave, but ... we have another long day tomorrow."

She knew she was well inside her agreements with Doug and Max. And Ananda and Ayala, although for some reason the women got jealous much less. But she was curious how gracefully he'd deal with stopping tonight—and even more, how he'd do tomorrow. It was OK if things were awkward, but the big question for her was how he faced the awkwardness.

He pulled back and said, "Whew!" He was smiling, and she felt the wave of slight concern she'd had drop. "Of course, of course. This has been lovely. Thank you. For all of it." Then: "Which isn't to say I'm not a bit sad you're heading out."

She turned him around and grabbed him from behind, running her hands over his chest than down lower, feeling him. "Me too. But it's better this way. Mmmmmm slow."

They went outside to the night, still muggy. He said, "Head out to the end of the dock, I'll have my driver come around."

"Ohhh, rich people." She gave him a peck, stepped off the boat and headed down the dock.

As soon as she got in the car she txted Doug, "dakota holy shit"

He wrote back, "ohhh boy. what now. any cute sailors in your evening?"

She wrote, "omg yes. remember the whole crazy dem capitalism

125

pilot project idea we had? from years ago?"

"hmm maybe. the new systems transformation one? the one we talked about doing offshore somewhere since california is too expensive"

"yeah yeah, so i gave them this quick overview of it and rafael says, 'what if money was no object.'"

Doug wrote, "wait who is them? where are you?"

She wrote, "ah yeah - i was at a dinner. bunch of funders and org people, on rafael's fucking megayacht. oh and erykah somethingorother, that crazy lady from powell's party. somehow"

There was a pause and she wondered if he was horribly triggered, or what. "looking it up" was all he wrote. Then a minute later, "woah, the renegade?"

"yup"

He wrote. "ummm woah. are you still there?"

"no, i left a minute ago."

"ok so did you make out"

She hesitated. Eek. She really, really hoped he was ok. "is ayala around?"

"haha. yeah, she's right here laying next to me reading these." Julietta thought, oh thank heaven and earth for other lovers.

"ok yeah we totally made out. it was hot but all we did was kiss. he's pretty cool. i talked you up. he's new to open."

He wrote back, "wow. go you!"

She said, "you ok? think max will be ok? don't tell him yet. how triggered are you."

He wrote, "not bad. probably more triggered by the boat than your make out session on it. mercy"

She laughed. "i love you."

He wrote, "so, what are you going to do? how'd you leave it?"

"well he's pretty interested. i pretty much told him out, but i'd give him some names of people who could lead it. i guess i could do

126

some of the initial research and setup it he insisted."

He said, "you really don't want to run it"

She wrote, "ugh. no. not again, not this soon after the campaign. plus i think he wants erykah to run it maybe."

He wrote, "oh ugh. will she fuck it up"

She wrote back, "shit." Long pause. She wrote again. "who knows. not my circus not my monkeys. unless rafael wants to bring me in"

He wrote, "well my guess is there's nobody better in the world for it than you. hate to say it but rafael probably agrees. i love you. go get some sleep and try not to wig."

She wrote, "ok i'll try. love you!!"

She got back to her room, still pretty wound up. She stripped off her clothes down to her soaked panties and started a bath. Her mind was racing, thinking about all the pieces that could be clicking into place. She got into the bath and immediately started to pleasure herself, but with a wave of fear rose alongside her excitement. When she came she was back in the crystalline vision she'd had with Ayala. She could see the renewal of things, see the new systems unfolding out from their plan. But as the orgasm shuddered through her system, the fear hit her like a wave right behind it and she sobbed and sobbed, at the effort and the thought of upping the stakes again and the sheer impossibility of something like this working. But she reassured herself she couldn't put her family through it again and went to bed, sure of nothing else but that.

Even with Ayala snuggled against him, Doug couldn't sleep. He stared at the ceiling in the darkness, replaying Julietta's texts in his mind and thinking about what her evening must have been like. He'd put up a good confident front for her, but the layers of stories started to kick in, about his disaster of a career, about what a threat to his relationship someone like Rafael represented. He caught himself. He knew that probably wasn't true, but the stories spun on and on in the darkness until eventually he fell into fitful sleep.

Back in her hotel room too, Erykah stared at her phone for a long while. She laughed to herself and said, "What the hell." She picked it up and texted Rafael, "you up? had some ideas about the campaign. want to keep talking?"

Rafel watched Julietta walk down the dock, as she got in the car his phone buzzed with the message from Erykah. He wrote her back, "sure. me too." He hesitated, watching as Julietta got in the car, then finished with "want to come here to the boat?"

And hit send.

ACKNOWLEDGMENTS

When I started writing this in 2013, I reckoned that attempting to write near-term speculative fiction about American democracy was most likely an act of incredible folly. It's proven to be vastly weirder than I ever would have imagined.

Only my family, friends and broader community have made this process survivable. An extensive list of everyone who has supported me through this would increase the download size of this book by too much, but two deserve particular mention: My wife, Jenifer Ancona, and my writing coach and structural editor, Tatyana Brown. There is no chance this book would exist without both of you believing in it and making an ongoing commitment to it that at times far outweighed my own.

Over 15 years of political activism and engagement, I've been lucky to know or hear the stories of a great many inspiring women. (and some inspiring men as well) Again, there are too many to list. But all of you have inspired me, and I hope you can see a fraction of your incandescence reflected in Julietta and the other characters here. Failing that, I hope you at least enjoy reading about a world waking up to just how amazing you are.

I'm grateful for the feedback (both positive and critical) of all my early readers. Caleb, David, Thor, Jenifer, Ellen, Shana, and Robert, your detailed feedback and thoughts were particularly helpful. Siân Gibby, thank you for your outstanding proofreading, for your invariably excellent word choice suggestions, and for the thousands of missing commas.

And last, an extra special thank you to the nearly 200 of you who contributed to the crowdfunding campaign. You improved the end product immeasurably, and your material support was part of what kept me going. I hope you enjoy reading, and I can't wait to hear what you think.

Abby Kearns
AJ Simon
Alissa Blackman
alixro
Amy Gavin
Amy Muller
anatshenker
Anca Mosoiu
Andrea Myers
Andy Johnson
annelisebreuning
annlarie
April Pedersen
Ariella Popple
Ashindi Maxton
Ben Kearns
brendan braybrook
Brian Goubeaux
Brian Leubitz
Bruce Buckheit

Caleb Donaldson
Cameron Burgess
Camron Assadi
Caryn Solly
Celia Alario
charles.chamberlain
Charlie Rebich
Cheryl Contee
Chris Messina
Colby Gutierrez-Kraybill
Colin Mutchler
Courtney Skott
Dale McGrew
Dale McGrew
Dan Girellini
Daniel F. Ancona III
Dave Meader
dave simon
david
Dawna Knapp
dawnrenee
Deanna Zandt
Deborah Dols
dhall
dmwinterhalter
doctorrooke
Don Ragland
drfun1969
eddie
Eddie Codel
Eden James
Edrie Irvine

Edward T. Ancona
Emi Gusukuma
Ellen Bravo
Ellen Steuer
Emily Toch
Erica C Payne
ertiepie
Favianna Rodriguez
Judith Zissman
George Feil
Heather Pritchard
Helen Ragland
Hillary Blackerby
James Home
James Rucker
Jason Oliver Mr Fantastic Reed
Jeanne Russell
Jen McGraw
Jenifer Ancona
Jennifer Blizard
Jennifer Burke
Jennifer Kain
Jeremy Bornstein
jeschumm
Joanna Burgess
joel
judillewis
Julie Chiron
Julie Fellom
Julie Lindsay
Justin Hall
karin.e.wertheim

Karl Banks
Katherine S Stuart
Kathryn Hack
Katy Stagl Thomas
kbarry
keridolsen
Kerry Smith
Kip Silverman
Kristen Kakos
Kristin Hull
Kristy Hilands
Lamont Lucas
Larry Ottinger
Laurel Gaddie
lchilders
Leah Kennedy
lucas oconnor
Lucie Moses
m_rickles
Manoj Dayaram
Marcy Swenson
Marea Goodman
Margaret Ancona
Marina Sennett
Mark Finnern
Mark Welch
Marty Sennett
Matthew Deans
mattsinger.mt
Melissa Michelson
Michael McGeary
Mike Sager

Miles Kurland
mjs-ecom
Molly Steenson
nadine
Natalie Foster
nikki
oceanrobbins
Olivia Carlson
Patrick Donohue
Patrick Kane
Patty Stagl
Paul Hashemi
pepomint
Raven Brooks
Rebecca Marshall
Richard Flacks
rjtmmc
Robert Cruickshank
Robert Lord
Rocky Mullin
rusty
Ruth Goldstone
shanajamessf
shane.king86
Shawna Jaquez
ssclark
stangri
Steve Phillips
Steve Simitzis
Stuart Trevelyan
Sumati Sparks
Tamara Draut

Tessa Levine
Timothy James
Tom Berger
Tori Ancona
Tracy Van Slyke
viola.toniolo
Walter Gray
Will Goldberg
William J Ancona
William Pietri
William Wimsatt
William Winters
Zach Larson

WHAT'S NEXT

Don't panic! The rest of the book is already written, and part 2 will be out very soon. Sign up to the email list and/or follow me on social media, and you'll be the first to know when part 2 is ready.

On the web at …
ReadVenusShrugged.com

On Twitter …
twitter.com/DanAncona

And on the Book of the Faces …
facebook.com/ReadVenusShrugged

Thanks so much for reading!
Dan
April 2017

Made in the USA
San Bernardino, CA
22 May 2017